GOD'S INVITATION TO BELONG AND BE LOVED

COME HOME

FOR TEEN GIRLS

CAROLINE SAUNDERS

Lifeway Press®
Brentwood, Tennessee

Published by Lifeway Press® • © 2024 Caroline Saunders

No part of this book may be reproduced or transmitted in any form or by any means, electronic or mechanical, including photocopying and recording, or by any information storage or retrieval system, except as may be expressly permitted in writing by the publisher. Requests for permission should be addressed in writing to Lifeway Press˚; 200 Powell Place, Suite 100; Brentwood, TN 37027-7707.

ISBN: 978-1-4300-8645-1 • Item: 005846183
Dewey decimal classification: 640
Subject headings: HOME \ HEAVEN \ JESUS CHRIST

Unless otherwise noted, all Scripture quotations are taken from the Christian Standard Bible®, Copyright © 2020 by Holman Bible Publishers. Used by permission. Christian Standard Bible® and CSB® are federally registered trademarks of Holman Bible Publishers. Scripture quotations marked (ESV) are taken from the the Holy Bible, English Standard Version® (ESV®) Copyright © 2001 by Crossway, a publishing ministry of Good News Publishers. All rights reserved. The ESV text may not be quoted in any publication made available to the public by a Creative Commons license. The ESV may not be translated in whole or in part into any other language. ESV Text Edition: 2016. Scripture quotations marked (NLT) are taken from the Holy Bible, New Living Translation, copyright ©1996, 2004, 2007, 2013, 2015 by Tyndale House Foundation. Used by permission of Tyndale House Publishers, Inc., Carol Stream, IL 60188. All rights reserved. Scripture quotations marked KJV are from the Holy Bible, King James Version.

To order additional copies of this resource, write to Lifeway Resources Customer Service; 200 Powell Place, Suite 100; Brentwood, TN 37027-7707; order online at www.lifeway.com; fax 615.251.5933; phone toll free 800.458.2772; or email orderentry@lifeway.com.

Printed in the United States of America

Lifeway Girls Bible Studies • Lifeway Resources
200 Powell Place, Suite 100 • Brentwood, TN 37027-7707

Cover design by Micah Kandros

Editorial Team,
Lifeway Women
Bible Studies

Becky Loyd
Director, Lifeway Women

Tina Boesch
Manager

Chelsea Waack
Production Leader

Mike Wakefield
Content Editor

Tessa Morrell
Production Editor

Lauren Ervin
Art Director

Sarah Hobbs
Graphic Designer

Editorial Team,
Lifeway Girls
Bible Studies

Chuck Peters
Director, Lifeway NextGen

Karen Daniel
Manager, Small Group Resources

Morgan Hawk
Content Editor

Stephanie Cross
Production Editor

Shiloh Stufflebeam
Graphic Designer

CONTENTS

ABOUT THE AUTHOR

Caroline Saunders is a writer, Bible teacher, pastor's wife, and mother of three who believes in taking Jesus seriously and being un-serious about nearly everything else. She loves to serve at her church (it's not just the donuts), and every year, she retells the Bible's big story at a women's retreat that she and her friends offer local women through their parachurch ministry, Story & Soul. She's had the joy of publishing two Bible studies for teen girls (*Good News: How to Know the Gospel and Live It* and *Better Than Life: How to Study the Bible and Like It*), two picture books for kids ages 4-8 (*The Story of Water* and *The Story of Home*), and two retellings of selected books of the Bible for elementary readers (*Sound the Alarm* and *Remarkable*). Find her writing, resources, and ridiculousness at WriterCaroline.com and on Instagram @writercaroline. (And finally, let it be known that Caroline's kids said, "Mom can make a joke out of anything," and so she ran and added that to her bio.)

DEDICATION

To the women of Story & Soul (especially my teammates and sisters Christin and Megan):

I wonder if you know how you have been home to me when I felt like I had nowhere to go? How I have tearfully praised God to watch as each December, the faces looking back at me grow to look more like family? Seeking God's Word on your behalf has been one of the greatest joys of my life. Thank you for enjoying His story with me. May this serve you.

WELCOME

In fall 2019, I committed to studying the theme of "home" in Scripture the following year. Of course, 2020 was, in many ways, all about home: we were trapped in our homes; we were separated from those who felt like home to us; and we became increasingly aware that this home didn't feel as safe as it once did. As disturbed as I was about the world, I marveled over all there was to uncover about home on the pages of the Bible. It starts with a perfect home and its tragic demise, contains story after story of people who aren't home yet, and offers God's promise to bring His children home. The more I studied, the more it became clear to me that "home" stretches far beyond a theological concept—it's deeply personal. I began to catch the scent of heavenly homesickness on every person I encountered.

Our lives have different shapes, and yet the longing for home takes up space in our hearts in a way that's both universal and seemingly impossible to describe. We all have our own ways to deal with this, like striving to make our current homes perfect or reaching back for old memories and happier times, hoping they hold the key to home.

But the Christ follower doesn't have to look around or look back to find home—she gets to look ahead. I wrote this study to root you in the truest story, to show you the Way (Jesus), and to help you walk by faith. After all, God has promised to bring His children home, and God always keeps His promises.

HOW *to use this study*

WELCOME!

We're so glad you've chosen to do this study! *Come Home* is a seven-session study in which Caroline Saunders follows the theme of home through the Bible. From humanity's first home to our eternal one, we'll see God drawing near to abide with us. We'll find that even the best aspects of home here are just a glimmer of what God is building for us through Christ. This study will affirm that our longing for home is good and purposeful, pointing us to our truest home which is found in Him.

GETTING STARTED

Because we believe discipleship happens best in community, we encourage you to do this study together in a group setting. Or, if you're doing this alone, consider enlisting a friend or two to go through it at the same time. This will give you friends to pray and connect with over coffee or through text so you can chat about what you're learning.

Here's a look at what you can expect to find in this study.

GROUP GUIDE

Each session begins with a Group Guide that allows you to begin your week together taking notes and asking questions to help you internalize and apply what you've read. If you're doing this alone, maybe ask a friend or your mom to do this part alongside you! We've included a mom and daughter guide on page 142 to help you get started.

PERSONAL STUDY

Each week features three days of personal study to help you trace the theme of home through Scripture. You'll find questions to help you understand and apply the text, plus insightful commentary to clarify your study.

LETTERS

Day 4 of each week features a letter that expresses the writer's personal experience with home. The authors of these letters are women from different walks of life. You'll have space to share how each letter resonated with you and helped you understand God's view of home.

POEMS

Caroline closes every week with a poem that captures the heart of the message for you to reflect on. The final poem of home—which includes a video read— is set apart on pages 144-149 due to mentions of grief and loss. Take care as you determine whether to read and watch.

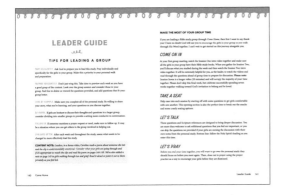

LEADING A GROUP?

You can locate a leader guide on page 140. The leader guide offers several tips and planning for each week. We've also provided intro videos to use as you're getting started. Instructions to access the videos can be found on page 160. To find additional resources for leaders, visit lifeway.com/comehome.

the

FIRST
HOME

session one

It was very good indeed.

GENESIS 1:31b

Home is hard to define, but we all know it when we see it, smell it, hear it—or when we miss it. Our stories are full of homesick moments, and maybe that's why we have a tendency to look back— to try and grab onto what we once had. But when we look at God's story of home in the Bible, it's clear that for the Christ follower, home is not behind. Home is ahead. We're all spiritually homesick, thinking we're longing for something we once had while actually longing for something we've yet to have, something promised to God's people.

In this week's study, we're going to look at the first home. God made it, and it was wonderful. But an enemy of home showed up, and soon, all hope of home seemed lost. However, God promised to defeat this enemy and make the way home.

GROUP GUIDE
session one

COME ON IN

Don't forget to watch the intro video as you're getting started. Instructions to access the videos can be found on page 160.

You probably decided to do this Bible study because you connected with the word *home*. It's a rich word that's hard to define, yet easy to recognize. It's a *place,* but not just a place! It's usually *people,* too, and there has to be a certain level of *peace* among the people for it to truly feel like home.

Home also affects our senses on every level. Something can sound, smell, or look like home. Home is a that particular blanket, the dog that barks for no reason, the way your mom makes a peanut butter and jelly sandwich.

How would you finish this statement "To me, home is . . ."?

One example of home in my life is the front door of our old house, which I'd painted yellow. When we moved, my then three-year-old daughter cried and said, "I want to go to the house with the yellow door!" What she meant was, "I'm homesick." My daughter's tears reveal another thing about home: our deeply felt belief that home ought to be *permanent*—and yet it never is.

Our natural tendency is to look back and try to grasp at things from our past. But when we look at God's story of home in the Bible, it's clear that home is ahead. We're all spiritually homesick, longing to belong and be loved. So if you're longing for home, you are in the right place! God's Word will show us the way because all of it points to Jesus, who called Himself "the way." He is the way, and He is the way home.

TAKE A SEAT

To begin our study of home, let's look at the first home.

READ GENESIS 1:1. The Bible starts with this summary statement, and then we get specifics: God says "Let there be" a bunch of times, and then, every time, the thing will be. God's word makes a way, always.

READ GENESIS 1:2-5.

> **What was the earth like in verse 2?**
>
> **What made the light come to be?**
>
> **How did God describe the light?**

Right away it's obvious that God creates good things, and He places them within life-giving boundaries. Regularly, the light will light, and regularly, it won't. (Night!) This was the day one of creation.

Genesis 1:6-25 tell us about days two through six of creation, and they follow a similar pattern: God tells a thing to "be," it does "be," and it is good. Nothing was blah—it was all beautiful and bountiful. It was also incredibly orderly. Over and over, God placed his new creation within life-giving boundaries. The sea had a place, and so did the sky. The sun had a place, and so did the moon. Through a series of "let there be," the world was filled with orderly awesomeness!

READ GENESIS 1:26-27. Before, God said, "Let there be," but now God said, "Let us make." Make is an artistry word! Humanity would be crafted with special care and intention and would be, somehow, like God. What an honor! (PS: If you look ahead to Genesis 2, you'll get to "zoom in" on when God created man and woman. When man met woman, he wrote a poem! They experienced God-designed, perfect togetherness.)

> **Look over Genesis 1:28-31, and whenever you see the word "every" in your Bible, circle it. How many times did you spot it? What does this tell you about God?**

The first people to hear the story of the first home were probably the Israelites that Moses led out of Egypt. (You can read about this in Exodus.) They would've been amazed by God! He wasn't like the gods they'd heard about in Egypt. He is God of everything! But they struggled to trust God on their long journey home. But God wasn't just leading them to a *place* but was forming them as a *people*. Maybe the story of the first home helped them understand the way home wasn't merely a path but a Person.

Describe man and woman's experience of home. (Think about the place, the people, and the peace they experienced.)

God is a God of abundance! He makes good things, and He gives them generously. I love that after all the creating, verse 30 says, "And it was so." Of course it was! God's word makes a way, always. By His word, God created a home—a place of peace and perfection—and its inhabitants.

How did God describe creation in verse 31?

If you're familiar with this part of the Bible, you know a plot twist is coming. As the events in Genesis 3 began, the serpent tried to chip away at that perfect togetherness and trust. If this was a different kind of story, Eve would've said, "Ah! A talking snake!" and she would have run away, and that would be the end. But Eve never had any reason to be suspicious before, so she chatted with the slithery guy. Let's analyze their conversation.

READ GENESIS 3:1-5.

How did the serpent (also known as Satan) tempt Eve to doubt God's goodness?

How does Satan tempt you to doubt God—to be suspicious of God's life-giving boundaries?

God created the whole world with His word, so it was pretty bold of the serpent (and man and woman) to doubt God's word. (In our personal study this week, we'll compare the serpent's words to God's words, because this is something we need to practice for our own lives.)

READ GENESIS 3:6-7.

What three things did Eve notice about the tree?

The first two things "good for food" and "delightful to look at" were true about all of the trees God had given them (Gen. 2:8-9). It was the third quality—wisdom—that tempted the woman. But wisdom isn't something that comes from a tree—it comes from God (Prov. 1:7). The more man and woman walked with God, the more they'd become wise.

What did man and woman choose?

What was the immediate impact?

In this part of the story, Adam and Eve probably had a feeling similar to that dream when you're naked in the school cafeteria. They try to cover themselves up, DIY-ing some clothes out of some leaves that would inevitably turn brown and shrivel and die and basically be the worst clothes ever. They thought eating the fruit was the path to good things—but it wasn't.

Adam and Eve had sinned. Sin is anytime we step outside of God's design. And sin is the ultimate enemy of home.

READ GENESIS 3:8-13.

Man and woman probably used to feel excited when they heard God coming. Now what did they feel?

Throughout this study, you'll hear me say that sin is the enemy of home. It is! Think about how pride, jealousy, selfishness, rage, and other sin rip at the fabric of our earthly homes. But know that behind sin is an enemy of God: The serpent, who we know as Satan. He introduced sin into the first home, and he wants nothing more than to tear down everything God calls good (Eph. 6:12). He will use lies and deception to influence us to choose destructive sin. But he will be crushed through the cross and empty tomb of the woman's offspring, Jesus Christ.

Why did man say they hid?

What kind of blaming do you notice in verses 12-13?

Sin entered this home like an intruder, destroying togetherness and trust and setting up shame, blame, and suspicion. Sin promises good stuff but can only deliver bad. But there's good news: God will always, always deal with sin.

Write Genesis 3:15 below.

This verse gives the first hint of God's plan to rescue this home! It promises the defeat of the serpent and his weapon of sin. The Eden promise is: *"The enemy of home will be destroyed."*

In your personal study this week, we'll learn more about this promise and how God dealt with sin in the garden that day. We'll get a better understanding of home's great enemy (sin), and how home will look with this enemy around.

READ GENESIS 3:21-24.

What did God provide for man and woman?

Why did man and woman have to leave the garden?

In one of the saddest moments in all of Scripture, Adam and Eve had to leave the garden God made for them. Because sin had made its home in their hearts, this home was no longer safe. The tree of life was there, and it would be disastrous for Adam and Eve to reach for this and live forever while soaked in sin! Once again, God offered a life-giving boundary. He is always good, and He would make the way home.

What does the goodness and abundance of the first home teach us about God? Does that challenge your thoughts on God in any way? Explain.

In what areas of your life do you currently see God's goodness on display?

How does this part of God's story provide hope for a current struggle?

If someone asked you what you learned in our time together today, what would you say?

LET'S PRAY

The first few chapters of Genesis help us see something at work in our own lives: sin is the enemy of home. In some way, we all have experienced this. As we end this time together, how can we pray for one another? Write down any prayer requests, and come back here throughout the week. As you pray, remember the promise of home ahead.

DAY ONE
THE GOOD HOMEMAKER

No one makes a home like God.

LOOK UP PROVERBS 3:19 AND HEBREWS 11:3 and write both verses below.

God built the first home with His word—with His wisdom! The first home was spectacularly lovely and jam-packed with the fruit of God's wisdom, crammed with evidence that God's word is powerful. The big theme here is *life*. God speaks life-giving words, offers life-giving boundaries, and even gives His creation the ability to create more life.

DAY ONE OF CREATION (GEN. 1:3-5) INTRODUCES US TO A PATTERN: GOD *SAYS*, GOD *SETS*, GOD *SHOWS*.

- God **said**, "Let there be light," and then, BOOM! there was light.

- He also **set** a life-giving boundary—sometimes the light would light (day), and sometimes the light would not (night).

- God **showed** His goodness. God called the light good, and of course it was.

This *says*, *sets*, *shows* pattern holds from days two through six of creation.

Read Genesis 1:6-25, and keep an eye out for the *says, sets, shows* pattern. Then, pick two of the days listed, and answer the questions below:

Day 2: Genesis 1:6-8

Day 3: Genesis 1:9-13

Day 4: Genesis 1:14-19

Day 5: Genesis 1:20-23

Day 6, before man:

Genesis 1:24-25

SOMETIMES GOD SHOWS HIS GOODNESS IN AN OBVIOUS WAY ("GOD SAW THAT IT WAS GOOD" IS SAID A LOT!), AND SOMETIMES THE GOODNESS IS IMPLIED BY THE BEAUTY AND BOUNTY OF HIS CREATION. THIS IS A REALLY COOL THING TO CONSIDER ABOUT GOD—HE DIDN'T HAVE TO MAKE THINGS WONDERFUL, BUT HE DID!

DAY _____

What did God *say*?

What boundary did God *set*?

How did God *show* His goodness?

DAY _____

What did God *say*?

What boundary did God *set*?

How did God *show* His goodness?

When you've finished paying attention to Genesis 1:6-25, check this box ☐. *(There's no reason for this except that we just love a box-checking moment.)*

Confession: I have this tendency to think of God as a grumpy, cross-armed principal with a clipboard where He writes down all the bad stuff I do. He might say, "Late again, I see," or "Well, I'll forgive you, but I'm not happy about it," or rattle off a bunch of rules designed to squash any fun I might be having.

Do you relate to this in any way? Explain.

BIBLE STUDY TIP:

IF YOU'RE COMFORTABLE WRITING IN YOUR BIBLE, YOU CAN LABEL THESE THINGS AS YOU READ THE PASSAGE. (FOR EXAMPLE, YOU COULD UNDERLINE THE WORDS GOD SAID, CIRCLE THE BOUNDARY GOD SET, AND ⭐ STAR THE GOODNESS GOD SHOWED.) AS YOU READ, YOU MAY WANT TO PLACE A QUESTION MARK ? BY ANYTHING THAT CONFUSES YOU. MAYBE A FUTURE STUDY DAY WILL ANSWER YOUR QUESTION, OR PERHAPS YOU CAN DISCUSS IT WITH YOUR GROUP WHEN YOU MEET.

The creation narrative (and probably every other part of the Bible) blows my wrong view of God to smithereens. It's clear His word is powerful, His boundaries are life-giving, and His goodness is evidenced everywhere. God isn't a grumpy principal we try to dodge in the hallways of life. He's an open-armed Homemaker whose home we want to run to!

What does the creation narrative teach you about God's words?

How does the creation narrative inform the way you view God's boundaries?

How does the creation narrative help you remember God's goodness?

Too often, we're tempted to be like Eve and think God is holding out on us (Gen. 3:1-7). But the Eden narrative resets our wonky inner compass. God is not just good—He's the author of good! God not only gives us our lives—He makes our lives lively! The first home equips us to wipe the smudge off our glasses and view the whole concept of home through a clearer lens. Truly, we can trust God's promises of home—because the whole notion of home has its origin in Him alone.

DAY TWO
THE TOGETHER HOME

Have you ever been in a home that looked great and had great stuff but you didn't really feel at home? Sometimes "perfect" homes can make us feel too human, like, *What if I spill something, and they get mad at me?*

But here's wonderful news: God made the first home *with humanity in mind!* God made a home where humans could be with Him, and it was every bit as wonderful as you can imagine.

> **LOOK UP THE FOLLOWING VERSES.** **How does each one help you understand God's purpose for creation?**
>
> **Psalm 115:16**
>
>
> **Isaiah 45:18**

We already know this narrative is about to go "nail polish on the white carpet," but before it does, let's once again soak in the goodness of this first home.

> **Pick two of the following verses, and explain how they show God's** *consideration* **for humanity and the** *closeness* **that was enjoyed in this first home.**
>
> **Genesis 1:29-30**   **Genesis 2:16-17**   **Genesis 2:23**
>
> **Genesis 2:8-9**   **Genesis 2:18**   **Genesis 2:25**

VERSE	CONSIDERATION How can you tell that God thoughtfully shaped this home for people?	CLOSENESS What details point to togetherness?

God created this home not just for Himself and not just for humanity. God created this home for humanity to be *with* Him.

But look, it's not like God was sitting around, twiddling His holy thumbs and wishing He had someone to hang out with. If you've ever heard the word *Trinity* at church, you may know this cool yet confusing thing about God: God is one, and yet God is three. God the Father, God the Son, and God the Spirit are one, yet because God is three Persons, God enjoys perfect closeness and community. The first home is not God inventing togetherness but inviting people into it!

What images, memories, or ideas come to your mind when you hear the word *togetherness*?

Why do you think togetherness matters?

LOOK UP GENESIS 3:8 **and write it below.**

This verse occurs after sin entered the picture, but it also gives us a glimpse of what garden of Eden togetherness might've been like. God was walking in the cool of the day; the man and woman heard Him.

That day, Adam and Eve hid. But it's clear that hadn't always been the case. The Hebrew word for God's action in this verse indicates this walking was God's normal habit.[1] We can't help but wonder how many moments of not hiding Adam and Eve enjoyed before sin intruded their hearts, unpacking its suitcase of shame and separation.

God designed home to be a place where people are considered and experience closeness with Him and one another. It makes sense that in our homes, we want to feel considered—like someone wants us to be there and made space for us. We want to feel closeness—like we are liked and loved, like we belong.

Where do you notice a longing for "garden togetherness" in your life?

How does God's story encourage you in your story?

DAY THREE
HOME'S ENEMY

When I was a teenager, someone broke into my grandparents' home, a place that was really special for me. No one was hurt, but I remember feeling violated when I heard the news. Who would dare to steal here? Couldn't they tell it was home? But thieves don't honor what is precious: they take it.

READ GENESIS 3:1-5.

Complete the chart by writing down the serpent's words. Then, compare them to God's words.

THE SERPENT'S WORDS	GOD'S WORDS
GENESIS 3:1 Did God really say, "You can't eat from any tree in the garden"?	**GENESIS 2:16-17a** And the Lᴏʀᴅ God commanded the man, "You are free to eat from any tree of the garden."
GENESIS 3:4	**GENESIS 2:17b** "You must not eat from the tree of the knowledge of good and evil, for on the day you eat from it, you will certainly die." [Notice that this boundary is life-giving, meant to keep them living as God designed!]
GENESIS 3:5	**GENESIS 1:26-27** "Let us make man in our image, according to our likeness."

The serpent invited Eve to doubt what God says; to feel suspicious of the boundaries God set; to question the goodness God has shown. The serpent placed doubt in her mind about whether God had really considered her. He attacked the home's closeness by implying that this home is not full of wonderful surprises but full of secrets. His message is something like, "God seems good—but He's actually keeping good stuff from you."

Have you ever encountered a message like this? If so, what was the situation and how did you respond?

God's word played a powerful role in the formation of the first home. What role did *disbelieving* God's word play in the corruption of the first home?

When do you notice you're prone to pay attention to Satan's words and ignore God's words?

Genesis 3:6 says, "The woman saw that the tree was (1) good for food and (2) delightful to look at, and (3) that it was desirable for obtaining wisdom" (numbers added). God Himself made the trees to have qualities 1 and 2 (Gen. 2:9). But (3) wisdom can only come from God (Prov. 9:10). If Eve wanted wisdom, she needed to follow God. Instead, she followed the serpent.

The serpent told man and woman that if they ate this fruit, their eyes would be opened (Gen. 3:5). But they didn't understand this uncovering wouldn't be exciting. It would be exposing, like a spotlight in the shower.

What do Adam and Eve do in Genesis 3:7 to address their shame? Do you think this actually helped?

Have you ever responded to your sin and shame in a similar fashion? Explain.

The theme of their home had been life, but now death seemed all around. They didn't immediately drop dead, but the process of death had begun, and their sin caused the venom of sin to begin to seep into the world's veins.

The rest of Genesis 3 is full of hiding, blame, and consequences for the serpent, Adam, and Eve. It reminds us over and over of what we already know: *Sin is the enemy of home.* Pride, jealousy, selfishness, rage, immorality, and other sin rips at the fabric of our earthly homes. But know that behind sin is an enemy of God: The serpent (also known as Satan, the devil, the deceiver, the accuser, etc.). He was the one who introduced sin into the first home, and he still works to tempt us to sin. We must be on guard against sin, always ready to recognize it as an enemy, as something that will bring death.

Is it hard to see sin as an enemy sometimes? Why?

How has sin been the enemy in your story of home?

The good news is that God will deal with this enemy. Within the serpent's consequences, God gave a promise to humanity.

LOOK UP GENESIS 3:15 **and write it below.**

God covered Adam and Eve's shame and sent them away from their once-perfect home, but one day, He would send a Child who would defeat the serpent and, therefore, sin. This is the Eden promise: *"The enemy of home will be destroyed."*

DAY FOUR

A SISTER'S STORY OF HOME

The creation narrative teaches us that we were made to be at home with God—and it also teaches us that the enemy of home is sin.

On the final study day of each week, I'll share with you a letter from a fellow sister in Christ. As she shares her story of home, I hope it will help you better understand God's story of home and help you feel less alone in your own story.

Dear Sister,

Home and the feeling of homesickness has always been kind of a theme in my life, and so has the feeling of not really belonging anywhere. I'm adopted from China, so that's probably where part of it comes from. I don't know for what reasons my biological parents gave me away or why I ended up in the orphanage. I don't feel Chinese since I was raised with Western values. But I also don't feel Dutch since I don't look the same as my Dutch family.

God blessed me by giving me the two loveliest parents. They raised me with their whole hearts and all the love they have. They also raised me in faith, letting me know I have a heavenly Father who watches over me and holds me in His hand and that I belong in His kingdom, as His daughter. He knows where I come from and for what reasons my life came to be, and He has been there with me all the time. I belong with Him as His daughter! :)

Like Psalm 139:13-14 (KJV) beautifully says: "For Thou hast possessed my reins: thou hast covered me in my mother's womb. I will praise thee; for I am fearfully and wonderfully made: Marvellous are Thy works; And that my soul knoweth right well."

Even though (if all is well) there are many things and people to love on earth, it's nothing close to how much God loves us and wants us with Him! That thought gives me so much strength and peace! We are wandering the earth but our home—our true home where we belong—is with Him.

God is great!

— JADE VAN DER ZALM,
illustrator, the Netherlands

JADE ILLUSTRATED MY CHILDREN'S BOOK, THE STORY OF HOME!

Use the space below (or your own journal) to respond to this letter. You may want to use the following questions to guide your response.

What thoughts and feelings are you experiencing as you consider this sister's story?

What from her letter most resonates with you and why?

How does her story help you remember God's invitation to belong and be loved?

THE FIRST HOME

In the beginning,
God used His word
To turn a bunch of nothing
Into land, sea, beasts, birds

Man was created by God
And was created for home
Look how God provided
Look how man was known

He made us to bear His image
To point the world to Him
At first this purpose seemed plenty
Until the deceiver stepped in

"Did God really say?"
The serpent questioned the Word
It made us start to wonder
Did we really hear what we heard?

Sin promised to give
But really it was a crook
It intruded our home
And took, and took, and took

God punished but promised
A Seed would be sown
To provide our salvation
To make our way home

SEEKING
a
HOMELAND

session two

By faith Abraham . . . went out,
even though he did not know where he was going.

HEBREWS 11:8

Sin made its home in every human heart, and yet God still desired
to be with people. He set His favor on one particular man—a
guy named Abraham—and gave Abraham a promise of home
that seemed impossible. Abraham didn't know where he was
going or what God was doing, but he believed God. Rather than
settle for a "perfect" earthly home, Abraham looked ahead to the
better home God promised. Abraham definitely wasn't a perfect
guy, but despite all his failings, God kept his promise to Abraham
and passed it down to his son, and his grandson, and his great
grandsons. Through this family we begin to see the way home that
God was building.

GROUP GUIDE

session two

COME ON IN

After sin entered the picture, it did what sin does: it grew. But God's promises never wavered. Home was not hopeless. This is especially obvious through God's favor on a man named Abraham and his family. Before we go there, let's walk the bridge from Eden to Abraham:

- In Genesis 4–5, we learn about Adam and Eve's children. Tragically, their first son murdered their second son. It started with jealousy, which seems small, but God warned of the danger of sin. Like his parents, the older brother ignored God's words and invited sin like a welcomed guest. He killed his brother in jealous rage. Eve had another son, Seth, and through his line came Noah.

- In Genesis 6–9, we read about Noah. During Noah's time, sin made its home in the hearts of people to the extent that "every inclination of the human mind was nothing but evil all the time" (Gen. 6:5). Like Cain, the people of Noah's day refused to treat sin like an enemy. Sin did what sin does—it grew, stole, killed, and destroyed. God addressed this enemy by sending a flood that killed everyone outside the ark.

- In Genesis 10–11, we read about the world's fresh start through Noah. Sin, preserved within the ark in the hearts of Noah and his family, began to grow. But God set His favor on a guy named Abram, whom He renamed Abraham.

This brings us to Genesis 12. The rest of Genesis is about Abraham's family.

TAKE A SEAT

Abram means "exalted father," but that probably felt like a mean joke. At seventy-five years old, he didn't have any kids. However, God promised something that seemed impossible.

READ GENESIS 12:1-4. **As you read, check off each thing God promised.**

☐ Land

☐ Nation: This goes beyond children, beyond family, to be a whole group of people sharing in the same identity.

☐ Blessing that goes both ways: Abram's family would be blessed by God, and Abram's family would bless the world. Blessing in the Bible is associated with life. God promised that Abram's family would experience life and extend it to others.

Later, God changed Abram's name to Abraham, which means "father of a multitude"—so we'll call him Abraham. The Abrahamic promises are these: *"I will give you a place, and I will make you a people who can both enjoy and pass along my blessing."*

Hebrews 11:8 gives us more insight into Abraham's faith. It says, "By faith Abraham . . . went out, even though he did not know where he was going."

How does it feel to not know where you're going? What does Abraham's example teach you about faith?

When Abraham was one hundred years old, he and his wife finally had a son, Isaac. (That's a long time to wait, isn't it?) Isaac had a son named Jacob, and God changed Jacob's name too: Israel.

Interestingly, Jacob was given this name because he "struggled with God" (Gen. 32:28). This "God fighting" tendency was a big theme in Jacob's life.[1] He inherited God's promises to his grandfather Abraham, but rather than believe and rest in the promises, Jacob schemed, plotted, cheated, and fought.

God's people have always had a tendency to fight to get their own blessings rather than trust God to do what He said. We want to get God's promises our own way rather than follow Him.

You may associate this name with the modern-day nation, but that is not what this study is about. We're focused on tracing God's promise of home through the Bible. Jacob/Israel began as man. Through that line, we can trace God's promise of home that extends all the way back to the redeemer God promised in Genesis 3:15. Whoa!

It's interesting that sneaky Jacob would be renamed Israel—a name that still lasts today, a name that has always reminded us of God's connection with people. The people featured in this study help us understand what it looks like to be a person who clings to God's promises—but more than that, they show us that God does not need perfect people for Him to be awesome. God will be awesome and will keep His promises no matter how sneaky and serpent-y the people behave.

How did Adam and Eve do this? Can you think of any other examples of this in the Bible?

Interestingly, despite how God's people struggled with Him and doubted His promises, God continued to come near sinners and fight for them. We see lots of verses in the Old Testament about this.

LOOK UP EXODUS 14:14 **and write it below.**

God is fighting for us and making the way home. We're invited to be still and trust Him. This is what we can think about when we hear the name "Israel" in God's story of home: God's people may put up a fight in good ways or bad ways, but ultimately, God is fighting for them.

One of the ways God fought for this family was by reminding them of His promises. Like Abraham, they often had to wait for a long time, didn't know where they were going, and didn't understand what God was doing.

Let's look at one of the repetitions of this promise in Genesis 28. In this scene, Jacob/Israel had fled home. (If you read the full story in Genesis 27, you won't feel that bad for Jacob. His own sneakiness had put his life in danger.) At nightfall, Jacob grabbed a rock for a pillow (ouch) and went to sleep. That's when God spoke to Jacob.

READ GENESIS 28:10-19.

How did God identify Himself?

In verses 13-14, God repeated the three things He promised to Abraham (land, nation, and a two-way blessing). But this time, there was a fourth thing.

Write verse 15 in the space below.

After his dream, what did Jacob say?

What did Jacob name this place? (Fun fact: *Bethel* means "house of God"; *El* meaning "God," and *beth* meaning "house."[2] If your name is Beth, we could call your house "Beth's beth.")

Jacob's dream featured a stairway (or some translations say ladder). Stairs make a way, so this stairway was like a visual aid to underline God's promises. God was making a way for them to be together. Moreover, God would come down and personally lead them home. Of course, God could have said "let there be" and this home would be, but that was not the way this time. The journey mattered! The journey with God is where we have the opportunity, like Adam and Eve, to decide that God's way is the good, life-giving way. It's where we have the opportunity to let God lead to His promises rather than scheme our way to them, like Jacob. Along the journey, God shapes us as we cling to His promises. Along the journey, we realize God wasn't just promising to bring His people home—His promise is to *be* our home!

The Abrahamic promises also include this: *"Wherever you are, I will be with you."*

Why is the journey home an important part of going home? What's your favorite part of the journey?

Of course, it's hard to go God's way. Any girl who knows Jesus personally will say she believes God's way is the life-giving way—and yet another part of her just doesn't buy it. This is normal on the journey home. It's evidence that we're not fully there yet, that sin still intrudes our hearts, and that we are in need of God's presence as we journey toward the place He's promised.

When do you struggle to believe that God's way is the life-giving way?

The book of Genesis ends with the story of Jacob/Israel's son, Joseph. Joseph was obviously his father's favorite, and his brothers were super jealous. Their envy almost turned to murder, like it did with Cain and Abel, but at the last minute, they sold their brother into slavery. Betrayed, Joseph wound up in Egypt in slavery and then in prison—but the Bible shows God's promises still stood.

LOOK UP GENESIS 39:2,21, AND 23. **What do they all say?**

Joseph was away from home by the most horrific of circumstances, but God was his home. By the time Joseph was an adult, food was scarce in the region, and people were dying. Israel's sons (Joseph's brothers) heard of a man far away in Egypt who had wisely stored away crops to provide for any who were hungry. Can you guess who this wise man was?

It was Joseph! At the end of Genesis, this broken family found their way back to one another, and a brother forgave the unforgivable and welcomed his family home. How was Joseph able to do this? Because God's promise to be with him had changed him.

READ GENESIS 50:15-22. **What stands out to you?**

Although Israel's sons were away from the land of God's promise, they experienced a glimmer of home. Their family was together, somehow preserved from the sin that had sought to devour them. God made the way!

Joseph's story (like Jacob/Israel, Isaac, and Abraham's stories) is a glimmer of a bigger story. One day, a Son would leave His glorious home. Through Him, the hungry would be saved and betrayers would become brothers.

LET'S TALK

Jacob had a life-changing encounter with God at Bethel. What is one Bethel moment you've had in your relationship with God? How did it impact you?

What does it mean that God was not just bringing Israel home but was being Israel's home? How is He doing the same for you?

Like Jacob/Israel, do you ever find yourself fighting to secure your own blessings rather than trusting God to keep His promises? Explain.

If someone asked you what you learned in our time together today, what would you say?

LET'S PRAY

There's lots of family conflict in this week's study. Family conflict can be one of the most painful parts of our stories of home. How can we pray for one another?

DAY ONE
OUR KEEPER AND THE PROMISE KEEPER

God offered Abraham (formerly known as Abram) a promise of home, and this big promise was made up of a few promises.

READ GENESIS 12:1-3. Look for the following three promises we tracked down in our group time, and check the box when you find each one.

☐ Land

☐ Nation

☐ Two-way blessing (Abram's family will be blessed; Abram's family will be a blessing)

Which promise appeals to you the most? Why?

These men lived a lot of life, and there had to be moments when it felt as if God was dragging His feet. But God's plans always unfold right on time and perfectly according to His promises. Over and over, God repeated these promises to Abraham, Abraham's son Isaac, and Isaac's son Jacob (later Israel) in passages like Genesis 12:7; 13:14-17; 15:1-13,18; 17:1-8,15-21; 26:2-6; 26:24; 28:13-15; 35:9-12. In other words, He repeated them A LOT!

Why do you think God repeated His promises so often?

Do you ever need to hear God's promises repeated? Why or why not?

Let's look at one of these repeated moments—the Bethel moment we encountered in our group time.

What was Jacob's response to God's promise?

Write verse 15 below.

This verse enhances the original promise to Abraham. This family would have God's attentive presence, His watchful gaze. God would be their keeper, their guardian. The Hebrew root of the word *shamar* means "to keep, watch, preserve."[3] Interestingly, we can also see this word in Genesis 4 in the story of Adam and Eve's oldest son Cain killing his brother, Abel.

READ GENESIS 4:9, **and write it below. Circle the word that you think is from the Hebrew root *shamar*.**

We hear the haunting echoes of Cain's word every time people hurt one another: "Am I my brother's keeper?" Am I supposed to "*shamar*" him?

This is why God's promise is good news: What people fail to do for one another, God does not fail to do. God's people have been clinging to this promise for generations. In fact, Psalm 121, which says in verse 5, "The LORD is your keeper" (ESV), was likely sung by travelers who looked to the distant hills of Jerusalem as they journeyed "home" to the city that held God's holy temple.

TAKE A MOMENT TO READ PSALM 121. **List a few ways this psalm describes God.**

Verse 7 says God will keep us from all evil. This can feel confusing because we all know God doesn't put a magical forcefield around us that makes us immune to sin's power and devastation. God isn't promising perfect safety at every moment: He's promising ultimate safety. God will be with us all our days and will bring us home to Him.

Think about the example of Jacob's son Joseph: God did not spare him from being sold by his brothers, or from being falsely accused, or from prison, but God was with him in the foreign land of Egypt. God placed His favor on Joseph again and again and used Joseph's position to rescue his family from starvation. Truly, the Lord was Joseph's keeper.

God's promise to keep careful and loving watch over His children still belongs to God's people today. And if we peek ahead at the story, it gets even better. Through Jesus, God will form a new family that will learn to love as God loves—a family of keepers (1 John 3:1,11-18).

Of course, God's children are not perfect keepers—not yet anyway. But God will keep us under His watchful gaze, growing us into His image until we are fully with Him forever.

DAY TWO
THE PROMISED HOME

Hebrews 11 is known as "The Faith Chapter"—a fun fact I learned in Bible Drill in elementary school. For lots of kids, Bible Drill is a fun, exciting program, but my attentive parents soon realized it was—how shall I say this—not for me. Competition is like a foreign substance in my body, and I am prone to allergic reactions. When asked to compete in any way, a little tornado swirls within me and threatens to come out. I suppose this explains the post-Bible Drill barfing.

I think I was worried my "perfect" image was at risk if I messed up. Interestingly, Hebrews 11 is a chapter jam-packed with people who were *not good enough* but who believed God's promises and found that He was good enough. Some Bible teachers have cleverly called this chapter "The Hall of Faith." It lists men and women from the Old Testament who responded to the Lord in faith. They are a "great cloud of witnesses" who encourage us to run the race set before us, looking to Jesus, the founder and perfecter of our faith (Heb. 12:1-2). Their example encourages us to look to Jesus and cling to God's promises.

READ HEBREWS 11:8-12 **and answer the following questions.**

When God called Abraham to go to a new place, God wasn't specific about the location. What do you imagine went through Abraham's heart and mind as he obeyed?

What kind of dwelling did Abraham, Isaac, and Jacob live in and why?

Who created the home Abraham was looking ahead to and how is that home described?

When Sarah looked at herself, she saw an old lady, making God's promises seem impossible. But when she looked to Him, what did she see?

Living in tents? Waiting on a baby as an elderly couple? When we look at our lives from a human perspective, God's promises make no sense. All we can see are the limits. But God Himself has no limits, and this is one of the reasons we can trust Him to fulfill His promises.

READ OVER HEBREWS 11:13-16.

God promised Abraham (1) land, (2) nation, and (2) blessing that goes both ways, but verse 13 reminds us that Abraham did not receive this in full while he was alive. Instead, he waved to God's promise from a distance and said, "My true home is ahead." Home was a guarantee—but not here, not yet. Rather than put all his hope in an immediate home, Abraham looked ahead to a better place.

Look back at the definition of faith in Hebrews 11:1. In your own words, describe how Abraham is an example of faith.

Everyone who belongs to the Lord is "seeking a homeland" (v. 14), like Abraham. How do you sense this seeking in your life?

Verse 13 talks about greeting the things God promised from a distance. But it can be challenging to trust God's promises when their fulfillment seems so far away.

How would you encourage someone struggling to trust God's future promises?

When verse 16 says Abraham and others desired a "better" place, the word *better* means "of a more excellent or effective type or quality."[4] By faith, we can long for what God alone has promised to His children: a forever-beautiful home with our forever-loving Father alongside our forever-loved family. It'll be better than anything we've ever experienced before!

If your home is hard, you can wave to the promises. Something better is ahead! Even if your home right now is wonderful, something better is ahead. Your true home is not here, not yet—but it is coming, and it's yours all the same.

DAY THREE
THE PROMISED OFFSPRING

We've seen how often God's promise of home was repeated to Abraham, Isaac, and Jacob—and it even pops up in the New Testament!

Let's consider what Paul wrote pretty firmly to the church of Galatia. They'd forgotten how the good news of Jesus works—that God's rescue for sinners comes by faith, not by people doing stuff. They thought following a specific Old Testament law (circumcision) was necessary for people to really be in God's family. Paul was like, "Um, no."

It's pretty easy to slip into this kind of thinking. Modern-day examples might be believing people need to act right before they can come to Christ, or believing people must read their Bibles, pray every day, and be baptized to truly belong to the Lord.

Paul, a fierce defender of the gospel, spoke to these Jewish Christians in a way they could understand—by bringing up Abraham. For these people, connection to Abraham was everything! After all, he was the original receiver of the promise. The twelve tribes of Israel descended from him. All Jewish people sought to trace their lineage back to one of those tribes of Israel (remember, Israel was Abraham's grandson). This would make each of them truly a part of the family—"Abraham's sons."

READ GALATIANS 3:5-9. **According to Paul, what makes someone truly one of "Abraham's sons"?**

According to Paul, God would give Abraham many, many offspring—but the promise would come through one offspring: Jesus (Gal. 3:16).

LOOK UP MATTHEW 1:1-16.

What three familiar names do you notice in verse 2?

What name finishes the family line in verse 16?

In Galatians 3:16, Paul claimed that the promise to Abraham would come through one offspring, Jesus. Matthew 1 helps us see exactly that. Don't miss this: God's promises to Abraham, Isaac, and Jacob are fulfilled in Jesus—He is the way that these promises are fulfilled to all of God's children. Through Jesus, anyone who looks to Him in faith can become a child of God and receive all of God's promises of home.

LOOK UP 2 CORINTHIANS 1:20 **and write it below.**

When we come across any of God's promises in the Bible, we can immediately think about Jesus. Jesus will help us understand the true meaning of God's promises.

When we don't view God's promises through Jesus, things can get tricky. We might think we belong to God because we behave a certain way—and maybe we'll treat people with different behaviors as outsiders. We might mistreat these "outsiders" or mislead them into thinking that to be part of the family, they have to act the way we want them to act.

Do you ever notice this kind of anti-gospel thinking within yourself, like Paul saw in the Galatians? Do you ever notice it within other Christians you know?

When we know that our true home is in God alone and that He is forming our true family, we are free to pursue relationships with people whom others are tempted to judge or overlook. Our social status is no longer the concern that it once was. Instead, we get to walk in confidence that we belong in God's family—and we get to extend a beautiful invitation to others: "Come home."

How can a better understanding of the gospel impact your relationship with God?

DAY FOUR
A SISTER'S STORY OF HOME

A big theme in this part of God's story of home is fractured relationships. People refuse to be one another's "keeper." Parents have favorites. Siblings hate one another. We get this! Our own fractured relationships reveal that we, like Abraham, Isaac, and Jacob, aren't home yet. But in faith, Abraham, Isaac, and Jacob waved at the promises ahead (Heb. 11:13).

I want to share with you a letter from a fellow sister in Christ. As she shares her story of home, I hope it will point you to God's story of home and help you wave to the promises ahead, in faith.

Dear Sister,

I once imagined home as a beautifully decorated house filled with necessities and sentimental items—fruit and family photos. Throughout my childhood, I lived the complete opposite. My place was anything but ideal. Anger, danger, fear, and sorrow settled in my living room. The space felt more like a house inhabited by wounded souls. Born in a dysfunctional home and hurt by broken people, I wished for better.

One day, I walked a winding Mississippi road littered with crunchy leaves while breathing in the autumn air. "What am I doing?" I asked myself. My legs had carried me out of my traumatic environment. I didn't know it, but I would enter a shelter later that evening. It would be a safe place with provision, helpful people, and rest. Tears would overfill my eyes when repeating the phrase "Temporary Home." It was both painful and relieving; I questioned, "Where is my forever home?"

By the grace of God, I was adopted into a family with sentimental photos, my face in several frames, and I freely grabbed bananas from the bowl of fruit on the counter. I had a God-fearing father who I knew would always protect and lead us. A mother whose love felt like ointment. Laughter, prayer, Bibles, and hugs filled the rooms. There, I received everything I had longed for in a home.

Each place taught me that earthly dwellings can yield both brokenness and beauty. But God with us is home here on earth and is a taste of the fullness to come. The most beautiful, comfortable home is flawed. We are all prone to sin and are in the hard and holy process of becoming more like Jesus. We journey through seasons of bliss and hardship. Yet, the God of hope walks us through every season.

The hoped-for home I desired in my youth changed with life's transitions. It became a college dorm, a shared house with roommates, a small upstairs room on a ranch, an even tinier room in a camper, and a cozy place with lots of space: many moves, yet God was with me.

Are you encountering the most overwhelming hardships of your life? Do you wonder why God would allow it? Are you unable to see the big story? God with you is home for now. Rest in this as you look forward to the glory of heaven. That home will have no sin, pain, sorrow, or trial.

Have you been blessed to experience the ideal home? Remember, there is much more. Let the gifts God has given you now point you to the delight of your eternal home.

May the trials and beauty of living the earthly experience lead you to the perfection of the new heavens and earth.

Where God is, there is home.

— JOSEPHINE D. ROSE, *writer and author of Talking to God, Mississippi*

JOSEPHINE LIVES NEAR ME AND IS ONE OF MY FAVORITE PEOPLE TO GET COFFEE WITH!

Use the space below (or your own journal) to respond to this letter. You may want to use the following questions to guide your response.

What thoughts and feelings are you experiencing as you consider this sister's story?

What from her letter most resonates with you and why?

How does her story help you remember God's invitation to belong and be loved?

SEEKING A HOMELAND

Outside of Eden
Sin grew
It changed what we did,
Corrupted what we knew

We invited the enemy
We entertained our foe
Until what God said was good
Didn't really seem so

We longed for home
Deep in our hearts,
But sin muddled the way
Infiltrating every part

God kept the course
While we waffled and waned
So prone to wander
Yet God stayed the same

He set His favor on Abram
Isaac and Jacob too
Their course filled with blessings
That affect me and you

It points to the Redeemer
The One God said He'd send
It points to our true home
Which we barely comprehend

Their days were a journey
And so, of course, are ours
We too live lives unsettled
Fighting against sin's power

But here's a big point
A promise to which we cling
God is with us always
It is a guaranteed thing

God does what He says
He always keeps His word
No matter how sin hisses
His promises are confirmed

It was true for them,
It's true for you;
God promised to bring us home,
That's exactly what He'll do

Going
HOME

session three

Lord, through all generations, you have been our home!

PSALM 90:1, NLT

Eventually Abraham's great-grandsons all wound up in Egypt. It's a long and dramatic story, but this is the detail you need for the story of home: Their family grew into a giant nation of people, and seeing them as a threat, Pharaoh enslaved them and sought to kill their sons. They were trapped in an unsafe home, but God was keeping watch. He offered miraculous protection to one of those baby boys, who grew to become the deliverer Pharaoh feared. His name was Moses. If there's anyone acquainted with the longing for home, it was him. Moses never really had a place to call home. Even when God's people were almost home to the promised land, Moses wasn't allowed to enter. But still, he penned these words in Psalm 90 (NLT): "Lord, through all the generations you have been our home!" One of the ways Moses experienced "home" was by meeting with God in the tabernacle, an Eden-reminiscent tent designed by God and built by men for the purpose of togetherness. Eventually, this tent became the temple, a permanent structure where God's presence would dwell in the promised land. This would be the closest to true home God's people had experienced since Eden.

GROUP GUIDE

session three

COME ON IN

When we closed last session, Joseph and his brothers had reconciled in a way that's only possible because of God. He made a way! This family lived in Egypt and grew and grew. The growing was a blessing—but it began to feel like a curse to the Egyptian ruler, Pharaoh.

> READ EXODUS 1:7-11, **and describe Pharaoh's plan.**

But God had a plan, too.

> READ EXODUS 2:24-25, **and write all the verbs associated with God.**

God had been keeping watch all along, but the verbs indicate it was time to act. God was about to bring His people home. Of course, God could have said, "Let there be," but that wasn't the way this time. The way was through a man named Moses.

TAKE A SEAT

Moses was born during a time when Pharaoh was afraid God's people would overpower him, so he commanded all baby boys be thrown into the Nile River. Thankfully, there were God-fearing people who believed it was more important to follow God than to follow Pharaoh.

> LOOK UP HEBREWS 11:23. **What does it say about Moses's parents?**

In faith, Moses's mother created a sort-of mini ark, tucked her precious baby inside, and placed the basket among the reeds along the river. God kept the baby safe until Pharaoh's daughter discovered Moses, felt compassion, and decided to raise the child. So, Moses's story of home was complicated: He was adopted as a young child, sent to live away from his family of origin, and raised by people who hated and harmed his people. As an adult, Moses spotted an Egyptian beating one of his people, so Moses killed him. (He clearly wanted to be a rescuer, but it didn't go well.) Word spread, and Moses escaped into the land of Midian.

Moses's life was characterized by *not* being at home. And yet, as we have seen, he wrote this in Psalm 90:1: "Lord, through all the generations you have been our home!" (NLT). What did Moses understand about God and home that we do not?

Let's look at two conversations Moses had with God, and along the way, I think we'll see why Moses transformed from a person who identified as a *stranger* to a person who identified as *home with God*.

CONVERSATION 1: **READ EXODUS 3:1-17.**

How did God identify Himself in verse 6?

What job did God give Moses (vv. 10,16)?

What question did Moses ask in verse 11?

What did God promise in verse 12?

What question did Moses ask in verse 13?

What did God promise in verse 17?

If you've done my study *Good News: How to Know the Gospel and Live It*, you've heard me teach about this name! Its translation and treatment is a bit complex and special, but the simplest way to think about it is as being constructed from the Hebrew phrase "I AM." You may have heard it as *Yahweh* or *Jehovah*. You'll notice this name in your Bible anytime you see the word LORD with a capital L and smaller capital letters for ORD.

God wouldn't just take His people *out* of this unsafe home—He would take them *to* a wonderful home. Even better, He would be with them every step!

Moses had two big concerns: *Who am I?* and *Who are You?* Notice God's answer to the first question: "I will be with you." Moses's identity could be rooted in God. Moses could do whatever God asked and go wherever God sent Him with faith not in himself but in God.

That brings us to Moses's other question. Who is this God who promised to be with Moses? In response, God told Moses His name: I AM WHO I AM.

A phrase like "I AM" is all about presence. It stretches our understanding of God to go beyond this moment into all moments. It reminds me of the term "space-time continuum" we sometimes hear in movies or in science classes.

I AM is I AM at any and every point in space and time. No matter what, when, or where, "I AM."

How do you think it impacted Moses to understand that no matter what, when, or where, God is?

Moses had another conversation with God that helps us see that I AM is more than a location thing—it's a character thing. It's not just about where He is—it's about what He's like!

Leading up to this conversation, Moses was exhausted from leading God's people. He didn't want to keep going unless he knew God was with them. He wanted more of God!

CONVERSATION 2: **READ EXODUS 34:5-7.**

According to verses 6-7a, God is compassionate and gracious, slow to anger and abounding in faithful love and truth, maintaining faithful love to a thousand generations. The rest of verse 7 helps us see God's relationship with sin. He forgives it, and He punishes it. It may be hard to imagine at this point how both can be true, but at the very least we learn this: Sin is a big deal to God, so He will always deal with it in one way or another. Sin will never be shrugged off or ignored. This is good news for His promises of home because sin is the enemy of home.

Think about the powerful implications we've learned about God through His name:

- In Antarctica tomorrow, God is compassionate; in Japan yesterday, God is compassionate. Seven years ago, God is compassionate; a hundred years from now God is compassionate.

- That time you did that really shameful thing that you don't want to talk about, God is compassionate.

- Right where I am typing this, God is compassionate. Even if you are reading this fifty years later, God is compassionate right where you are sitting.

With these two conversations and Moses's history in mind, why do you think Moses called God "home" in Psalm 90:1?

Through Moses, God brought His people out of the unsafe home in Egypt, but He didn't bring them directly to the good home, the promised land. God led His people out of Egypt and to Mount Sinai, where God kept them for about a year.[1] It seems as if God was preparing His people for home. Through God's meetings with Moses, God instructed His people in His Word and His ways.

These are the promises of home we learn from this part of the narrative: *"I want to be with you. I will lead you home."*

The time in the wilderness required faith. God's people had to trust Him. But when they arrived just outside of the promised land, they sent a few men in to explore the land, and most came back terrified of the warriors who lived there.

READ NUMBERS 14:2-4.

What shocking thing do the Israelites wish for (v. 2)?

How can you tell the Israelites had totally forgotten about I AM's character?

The promise of home was just ahead, something they could literally wave to, but after everything God had done and everything they'd seen, they forgot I AM's presence and power! Sin once again proved to be the enemy of home.

God actually threatened to give up on them and make a greater nation through Moses. Of course, God could have done that, but I think He was setting Moses up to be an intercessor—a middle man, a go-between—for His people. Sin disorients people, and sinful people are in need of an intercessor to show them the way. How else will they get home? Moses was modeling something bigger—Jesus, the One who would intercede for sinners to make the way for them to be with God, to be home.

READ NUMBERS 14:18-25.

How can you tell Moses had not forgotten about I AM's character?

How did God respond to Moses?

What was the consequence for the Israelites' faithlessness?

That short stint in the wilderness turned into a forty-year journey. I can't help but feel for Moses here. He was so close to a physical home! Interestingly, Moses probably wrote Psalm 90 during this part of his life.[2] Moses's song is full of beautiful words, but it also has verses that are less quotable than we'd like. It reminds us that God has no limits, but humans have a lot of them. All of it shows a man's love for and faith in God. Moses asks God, "Satisfy us each morning with your unfailing love, so we may sing for joy to the end of our lives" (v. 14, NLT). This is the promise of home we learn from Moses: *"Home is where I AM is."* If we have Him, we have home.

The next generation finally entered into the promised land under Joshua's leadership. Eventually, they built a temple, which was a more permanent version of the tabernacle where God could live among them. It might feel like a happy ending—until you remember that sin was still growing. (More on all of this in our personal study!) But for now, know this: the Moses, tabernacle, and temple promises are these: *"I want to be with you. I will lead you home. Home is where I AM is."*

LET'S TALK

How was Moses's relationship with home complicated? Would you say you've had a complicated relationship with home? Explain.

If your group has time, you might read Psalm 90 together. The NLT translation uses the word "home" in verse 1, and other translations use phrases like "dwelling place" (ESV) and "refuge" (CSB).

God told Moses His name is "I AM WHO I AM." How would you explain what that means and how that name shapes the way you see God?

How have you experienced God's compassion and faithful love in recent days?

What are some things that keep us from trusting God when He's calling us to move forward in life, home, ministry? Are you currently struggling with any of these? Explain.

LET'S PRAY

Like Moses, all too often our desire for home doesn't match up with our experiences. God's promises are true for us, and we can wave to them in faith (Heb. 11:13). How can we pray for one another to have faith in the midst of our complicated home stories?

DAY ONE
TOGETHERNESS WITH GOD

After God's people were delivered from slavery in Egypt, they camped at Mount Sinai for a bit. Moses had gone up the mountain to receive from God the law (Ex. 24:12). These instructions were rooted in God's promise of home: They showed how the nation should live in the land they would possess. It would *bless* them and allow them to *be a blessing*.

But receiving those instructions took a while. "The people saw that Moses delayed" (32:1) coming down from the mountain, and they became what I call "spiritually itchy." *Where was Moses? What was God doing? Who would lead them?*

Rather than cling to God's promises, the people created a god that made more sense to them: a golden calf, made from their own jewelry. Then they got busy worshiping it, probably mimicking the worship of the Egyptians, who they'd witnessed for hundreds of years.

Culturally, this makes no sense to us, but spiritually, it absolutely does. They were uncomfortable with trusting God to make the way, so they made their own way.

How have you experienced this in your life?

When God told Moses what the people were doing, Moses acted as an intercessor or "middle man." (This foreshadows Jesus and is similar to the Numbers 14 passage we talked about in the group time. Flip back to page 54 if you want a refresher.)

READ EXODUS 32:9-14. What do you notice about how Moses interceded for the people?

Moses interceded by appealing to God's character, reputation, and promises. In response, God didn't destroy the people, but there were major consequences: death and sickness. But there was something else that got everyone upset. What could be worse than death and sickness?

READ EXODUS 33:1-4.

What was the devastating news God gave Moses, and how was it described (vv. 3-4)? (You may want to look it up in a few translations.)

How did the people react to the news?

God's people made it clear they didn't want to be led by God, so in a sense, God was saying, "Okay, fine. Go with your made-up gods." But the people quickly realized they didn't want God's promises without God's presence!

Do you ever want God's promises without God's presence? If so, why?

But once again, Moses interceded.

LOOK UP EXODUS 33:15 **and write it below.**

This is an important lesson about home. Without God's presence, the stuff God promises loses its sweetness. It's just stuff. Home is where I AM is!

How does this challenge your view of home?

In your life, what does it look like to value God's presence above all else?

Just after this, Moses asked God to show him His glory. He wanted more of God! So, God agreed. He gave Moses a small peek of His goodness and glory—and part of this was declaring His name, "I AM," alongside a list of character traits. If you ever forget what God is like, this is a text to remember.

LOOK UP EXODUS 34:6-7, **and highlight the verses in your Bible.**

Take some time to pray and thank God for being who He is. Ask Him to help you see areas in your life where you've chosen to follow a "god" you're more comfortable with. Ask Him to help you know Him more.

DAY TWO
CARRIED BY GOD

Did you know that God didn't allow Moses to enter the promised land because of Moses's sin? I have always found this a little upsetting and definitely confusing, especially because Moses's sin can seem, well, not that bad. (*Isn't it interesting when that's our reaction to sin?*)

Here's what happened: Previously, God had provided water for the Israelites by telling Moses (alongside his brother and co-leader Aaron) to strike a rock. When Moses did, water sprung forth from the rock. During a second incident, God told Moses to *speak* to a rock. Moses didn't speak—he struck. Moreover, before he struck the rock, he said this, "Listen, you rebels! Must *we* bring water out of this rock for you?" (Num. 20:10, emphasis added). Doesn't it sound like Moses was suggesting that he and Aaron were the ones providing the water?

God alone knows Moses's heart, but the Bible helps us see that at the very least, Moses disobeyed God and desired credit for something God alone could do. Moses was leading a nation who struggled to credit God for His works, so this particular kind of disobedience was dangerous. God doesn't shrug off sin—even when the important Bible guys are the offenders.

So, Moses couldn't have this earthly home. But you know what? Moses knew God, and because of that, Moses had something better than any earthly home can provide. And of course, he experienced this even more fully when he died and was welcomed into God's presence in heaven!

Before Moses died, he offered some final words to the nation of people, which you can read about in the book of Deuteronomy. This group of people were the now-grown children of those who had rejected God in the wilderness. Moses told this new generation of their people's history of faithlessness—and of God's faithfulness. He said, "The LORD your God carried you as a man carries his son all along the way you traveled until you reached this place" (Deut. 1:31).

In your own words, describe what it is like to be carried.

LOOK UP DEUTERONOMY 30:19-20. **Why do you think Moses said this to the new generation?**

Their parents had not chosen God's ways and thus, not chosen life. But this new generation had an opportunity to follow the Father's ways rather than their fathers' ways. To thrive in their new home, they needed to love the Lord—the Life-Giver—with their whole hearts.

LOOK UP ISAIAH 46:3-4.

Who was God talking to through the prophet Isaiah, and what was His promise to them?

What does this teach you about God's character?

Dear sister, your Keeper cares for and carries you. When you struggle to follow His Word, cling to His character. He is compassionate and gracious, slow to anger and abounding in faithful love and truth. He is the Life-Giver whose way is life! Remember that though the story of home in Scripture zigs and zags, every angle points to God's faithfulness. This is true in your story, too.

DAY THREE
THE TABERNACLE AND THE TEMPLE

We know the bad home moments invite us to cling to God's promises of home, but the good home moments do, too. The good things we've experienced are like movie previews, breadcrumbs, menu descriptions, neon arrows (pick your favorite metaphor) pointing us home.

Two important biblical "previews" are the tabernacle and the temple. Both were worship spots and places where God's glory would literally settle in and remind the people that God was with them. The tabernacle was a movable tent-like place that was used during the wilderness years and in the promised land until the time of King Solomon. The temple was a "permanent" building built by King Solomon in the promised land.

TABERNACLE

READ EXODUS 25:8. **What was God's purpose for the tabernacle He designed?**

We could spend hours studying the tabernacle's design. (Fifty chapters in the Bible are about the tabernacle![3]) All the details taught God's people about God—and the end result of the tabernacle allowed God's people to meet with God through their mediators, Moses and the priests. The tabernacle pointed back to Eden, and it also pointed ahead to Jesus. (More on that later!)

TEMPLE

When David was king, he realized that though he lived in a palace, God still dwelled in a tent. He wanted to build God a house, but God said David's son would be the one to build it. So David's son, Solomon, did. The dedication was a moment when God's people probably thought, "He did it! God did everything He said He would do. He's with us! We're home!"

After all, God's people had spent years wandering in the wilderness, longing for the comforts of home. Then they'd spent years enjoying the comforts of home in the promised land—but unfortunately, they became numb to the Lord, and sin was still the same enemy it was in the wilderness.

But by this point of King Solomon's reign, things were swelling like a song leading up to the bridge, like a blueberry so ripe it's about to fall right off the bush. Abraham's descendants were a *nation*, had the promised *land*, were enjoying great *blessings,* and were blessing others around them. More than that, God was with them, and they knew it.

READ 1 KINGS 8:1-11,17-20.

What happened when the priests came out of the holy place in the temple?

What does this passage teach you about God's glory?

How was God's promise to David fulfilled?

In this scene, David's son Solomon was dedicating the long-awaited dwelling place for the Lord. David didn't live to see this moment, but God always keeps His promises.

NOW READ 1 KINGS 8:27-30.

What do you learn about God's limitlessness in this passage?

How did Solomon appeal to God as the Keeper, who keeps a watchful eye on His people?

What do you think it means for God's name to dwell in this place? What was Solomon asking of God? *(Hint: Remember Exodus 34:6b-7.)*

What did Solomon ask God to do if people prayed toward this place?

There's talk of God's name dwelling here, which can seem kind of weird. But remember, God's name is more than just a label—it represents who He is. This temple wouldn't just belong to the Lord; it would point to His character. It would help His people remember what He is like and worship Him as He actually is. When God's people looked or prayed toward the temple, they could remember His compassion and graciousness, His slowness to anger, His faithful love.

It was incredible! But though this glorious moment seemed like a beautiful ending, it was just a temporary upswing. Sin was still the enemy of home. The worst was yet to come—but, because God keeps His promises, so was the best.

DAY FOUR
A SISTER'S STORY OF HOME

A big theme in this part of God's story of home is the importance of God's presence. It's a vital part of His promises. Home simply isn't home without Him. As Elizabeth Woodson says, "God's character shows us that His promises are true and will be fulfilled. The promises of God serve as a powerful lifeline during seasons of longing."[4]

I want to share with you a letter from a fellow sister in Christ. As she shares her story of home, I hope it'll point you to God's story of home and help you feel less alone in your story.

Dear Friend,

Have you ever anticipated an adventurous evening away from home, only to have some unexpected twist ruin your plans? If so, that may have left you "stuck at home," which probably didn't feel like your favorite place in that moment. That's exactly how I felt after my family's missionary assignment to Japan fell through, and I realized we'd be "stuck" indefinitely in Tennessee.

Don't get me wrong. I love my southern home, but after years of sacrifice and preparation, we were really looking forward to life abroad. The disappointment and hurt I experienced ignited a series of questions in my heart, like "How do I love my home when I don't want to be here?" It wasn't the "home" I envisioned.

After confessing all my bitterness and anger to God, in time, I remembered that God works all things for the good of those who love Him and are called according to His purpose (Rom. 8:28). So I decided that I would let go of the home that might've been to love the home that God gave me right then. That looked like living fully right where I was without holding back in anticipation of the next season.

Before this decision, my home was half-lived in. I just barely decorated because we were renting. I saw where I was as temporary, looking to the future overseas where I'd lay down my roots and connect with my neighbors. Though I mention my physical home, this mindset definitely carried into my relationships with my family and community. I was too half-invested to enjoy and live fully with them in the present.

But now, with new eyes and a renewed sense of gratitude, I can honestly say I love this unplanned home and community. Being present with my family as we are, where we are—not as I wanted us to be—has helped me realize the goodness we have here and how I share God's love with my family and neighbors. After all, how could I love a home abroad if I can't love my home right here?

Whatever your home looks or feels like, I think we can all relate to living a reality in our homes that we hadn't wanted or anticipated. When home isn't what we envisioned, can we trust God to give us peace and, dare I say, joy in those situations?

Yes, sweet friend. I'm a witness to that. If loving the home you have is a struggle right now, I'm praying that however loving your home looks in your life, you can bring your disappointment to God. Next, I pray that your honesty and yielded heart would lead to open eyes to see what good God is working in your home right now.

With much love,

— TITANIA PAIGE, *speaker and author of Come Home: A Redemptive Roadmap from Lust Back to Christ*

NIA AND I LOVE TO GET TOGETHER TO TALK ABOUT THE LORD AND WRITING WHILE OUR KIDS PLAY!

Use the space below (or your own journal) to respond to this letter. You may want to use the following questions to guide your response.

What thoughts and feelings are you experiencing as you consider this sister's story?

What from her letter most resonates with you and why?

How does her story help you remember God's invitation to belong and be loved?

GOING HOME

Trapped in an unsafe home
Mistreated and hurt
God's people cried out
And their Keeper, He heard

Through all those years
Of longing for escape
It was finally time
God made a way

It started with a baby
In the water placed
A son surrendered
By another raised

He often felt alone
Cause the home he knows is
His enemy's home
You know him; it's Moses

He fled once in fear
And Pharaoh didn't lament him
But he returned, God with Him
He returned 'cause God sent him

God's people were freed
From external oppressors
But the enemy within
Kept them chained as transgressors

This kept them from home
This too was unsafe
God spoke, and they scoffed
Anti-God, anti-faith

So the promise was given
To the next generation
They would be the receivers
Of land, blessing, and nation

But even in the days
Of God's presence and temple
It was never that pure
It was never that simple

Sin kept winning
They rarely fought it
They heard sin's lies
They indulged it; they bought it

The worst is to come
Tempting us to despair
Why so easy to wander?
To believe God doesn't care?

No matter what comes
The Bible's clearly shown
God is still I AM
He will bring His people home

Away
FROM
HOME

session four

*By the rivers of Babylon—
there we sat down and wept
when we remembered Zion.*

PSALM 137:1

God's people were finally home in the promised land, and you'd think it'd be smooth sailing—a "happily ever after" kind of thing. But they continuously welcomed the enemy of home—sin—into their hearts. God sent what seems like zillions of prophets to sound an alarm—like the kind that tells you when someone is breaking and entering. But God's people didn't care. They couldn't and wouldn't see sin as an enemy. So, God did what He said He would do: He sent physical enemies into the land to remove the people from their home. They went into exile. Far away from all that was familiar, God's people had to grapple with the physical evidence of what had been spiritually true for a long time: they were not at home with God.

GROUP GUIDE

session four

COME ON IN

Last session, we talked about King Solomon, who built a "house for the Lord"—a temple. On the day the temple was dedicated, Solomon prayed and described a situation to God: What if your people break your law? Will you forgive them if they look to you with truly repentant hearts?

Graciously, God answered yes (2 Chron. 7:14). But God warned that if they *persisted* in their sin—if they kept running toward sin and loving their sin—home wouldn't stay. Home is where I AM is, so when we love sin and the serpent's way more than God and His ways, home can't truly exist.

> **What's the difference between being a person who sins and being a person who persists in sin?**

If God's people kept running toward and loving their sin, God said He would take His people from this land, and He would even reject the temple itself (1 Kings 9:6-9). A place of glory would become a place of grossness.

But of course, God's people didn't listen. Here's what happened:

1. **When Solomon's son became king, Israel was sliced into two pieces: the Northern Kingdom of Israel and the Southern Kingdom of Judah.**

2. **Over the centuries, a few kings tried to lead the people in God's ways, but most kings led the people further into sin.**

3. **God faithfully warned His people through prophets. (You can read these warnings in books like Deuteronomy, Micah, Habakkuk, Isaiah, and Jeremiah.) Prophets were like alarm systems for this home, alerting of the danger of sin. The main message of the prophets was: *repent!* God loves to forgive repentant sinners.**

4. Like many of us when we hear alarms, God's people hit the snooze.

5. The Northern Kingdom of Israel was overtaken by the Assyrians in 722 BC. For about a century, the Southern Kingdom, Judah, thought, *that won't happen to us.* But it did.

6. The prophet Ezekiel (whom some scholars believe suffered deep trauma because of the exile)[1] and others were exiled to Babylon in 597 BC. Ezekiel had a vision of God's glory leaving the temple. (More on that in a bit!)

7. There were a few other stages of this exile, and then the capital city Jerusalem fell to the Babylonians in 586 BC.[2] The temple was destroyed, and all hope for home seemed lost.

This "away from home" season is called exile. It may be one of the most devastating and traumatic events in the history of God's people, but we don't talk about it much—maybe because it's so uncomfortable! After all, God caused the exile as a consequence for sin (Hab. 1:6). We can't help but wonder, was it okay that God did this? Plus, it's kind of hard to figure out who the good guys and bad guys are in this part of the story. The rescue was muddy, too. When God's people finally went back to the promised land decades later, it didn't really feel like home anymore.

> Do you ever feel like your story is confusing? Is it ever hard for you to figure out what God is doing?

We can't edit out the unsavory parts of our own stories, so let's not ignore this part of the biblical story either.

TAKE A SEAT

Before the temple was destroyed, Ezekiel had a vision of God's glory leaving the temple (Ezek. 9–10). This was just about the worst thing that could have happened because God's glory was the thing that made home home. It's hard to define "God's glory," but David Guzik describes it as "the radiant outshining of His character and presence."[3] When God shows up in big way, that place becomes a glory place!

Think about the "glory places" we've seen so far in this story:

1. The garden of Eden was a glory place where humanity walked with God.

2. When God had His people build the tabernacle, His glory would descend on it like a cloud. If the glory stayed put, God's people stayed put. If the glory went forward, the people followed (Ex. 40:34-38).

3. When King Solomon dedicated the temple, God's glory descended on it with a *whoosh*, perhaps literally knocking the priests off their feet (1 Kings 8:11). Then there was an epic celebration in which God's people "blessed the king and went to their homes rejoicing and with happy hearts for all the goodness that the LORD had done for his servant David and for his people Israel" (1 Kings 8:66). At home in the promised land, God's people could look to this "glory place" to remember who God is, what He'd done, what He'd promised, and that they were His.

   Can you think of any other "glory places" you've read or heard about in the Bible?

God's glory is the ultimate welcome mat, the ultimate "stay put" sign! It said, "God is here. It is time to stay. You are home."

LOOK UP JEREMIAH 2:11. **What did God's people exchange God's glory for?**

Sometimes in the Bible (and in life), God gives people what they want—not as a gift, but as a consequence. God's people made it clear that they didn't want Him. So, God had enemies to take them away from their homes, and then God's glory packed up and left, too. God's people were far from home by God's design—and even if they were able to get back, God's glory wasn't there anymore. God had removed the ultimate "stay put" sign, the ultimate welcome mat.

If you're wondering how this felt for God's people, the answer is . . . *not good*. Remember the sudden shame Adam and Eve felt after they got what they wanted from the tree of knowledge of good and evil? Perhaps the exile experience was like that. Maybe God's people realized what a terrible trade they had made by exchanging God's glory for idols.

This part of the story is characterized by homesickness.

Have you ever felt homesick? Describe the feeling. What happened that made you feel that way?

Here's a story that may be familiar to you but that you might not realize happened during exile: Daniel and the lion's den. Daniel was a young man taken from his home and forced to serve in the king's court in Babylon. But, like Joseph centuries before him, God was with Daniel and blessed him. Out of jealousy, many of the Babylonians plotted to trap Daniel so the king would stop treating him so well. Realizing the only way to trap Daniel was through his God, Daniel's enemies tricked the king into creating a law that meant anyone who prayed to anyone other than the king would be forced into the lion's den— where death would certainly await.

LOOK UP DANIEL 6:10. What did Daniel do when he heard about this new law?

How can you tell this kind of praying was a habit for Daniel in Babylon?

Where did Daniel face as he prayed?

Praying toward Jerusalem was not a superstitious thing—it was a faith-filled action! Praying toward the temple (or the place where the temple once stood) was a way for a person to remember God and His promises. Look up 1 Kings 8:48-49 to see some really interesting wording from King Solomon's temple's dedication prayer centuries before.

> **What similarities do you see between this prayer and Daniel's situation?**

Whoa, right? Daniel was banking on God's yes answer to Solomon's prayer. He had faith that even away from home, God would hear him. And of course, God did. He is I AM! When Daniel was busted for praying and sent to his certain death by being thrown into a pit of hungry lions, God miraculously rescued Daniel by shutting the lions' mouths.

But look again at 1 Kings 8:48. Though Daniel seemed to follow God with his whole heart, God's people as a whole couldn't seem to fully return to Him. They needed to repent (to turn from their sin and turn toward God), and they needed to stick with their repentance. But they kept running back to their sin. Sound familiar?

Amazingly, I AM is I AM always, even when we run to our sin. God had a plan to turn His people into people who could truly repent and be at home with Him.

> LOOK UP EZEKIEL 36:24-28, **and list the things God promised to the exiles.**

One day, God would perform a "heart transplant" of sorts. He would give His people a new Spirit—His Spirit—who would help them obey. God would bring them home by bringing Himself to dwell in them. He would bring them home by remaking their hearts. The exile promise is this: *"I will give you new hearts, and I will bring you home."*

Do you think God treated the people of Israel too harshly with the exile? Explain.

In those times when sin was having its way in your life, how did God get your attention and call you back to Him?

What strikes you the most about Daniel's prayer in Daniel 6:10? How should his prayer shape your own prayer life?

How does this uncomfortable part of the story of God's people encourage you to cling to Him in the uncomfortable parts of your story?

LET'S PRAY

God's people were away from home, feeling alone, rejected, confused. Maybe you relate to this. Maybe it seems God has broken every promise He's ever made. In times of spiritual dizziness, God's story can put us back on our feet. It reminds us that we can pray to God in faith, like Daniel. We can remember He is I AM always, even when we're far from home. He will certainly bring His people home, by recreating our hearts to fully know and love Him.

If you're comfortable, share an area in your life in which you need God's hope. Then, read Lamentations 3:19-24 together (which was likely written by the prophet Jeremiah during this time period), and use those words to pray for one another.

DAY ONE
GOD'S PRESENCE—GONE

As we talked about in our teaching session, when Ezekiel was in exile, he saw a vision of God's glory leaving the temple (Ezek. 10–12). This was a big deal, because God's people thought they'd be going home soon. They couldn't (and wouldn't) see that their sin was a big deal. They were worried about their outer reality, but God was concerned about their inner reality. They were not "home" with him because they'd let sin make its home in their hearts.

Have you ever had a season in which you intentionally ignored your sin? If so, describe it.

In what kind of situations do you think people are most likely to feel numb to God's Word?

In a sin-sick world, it can be challenging to think of sin as a big deal or to admit that we've sinned. Why is it important for us to understand and acknowledge that we've sinned?

Unfortunately, many false prophets pretended to have heard from God and told the people exactly what they wanted to hear.

LOOK UP JEREMIAH 23:16-32.

What message were the false prophets spreading (v. 17)?

What message did God actually send through His true prophets (v. 22)?

How does this passage reveal that God Himself brought about the exile?

What does this passage teach us about God's character?

God's people wanted peace without the God of peace. God's people wanted peace while making war against God with their sin. The false prophets gave them the permission to continue living the way they wanted—but when we follow our wants, we often end up somewhere we never wanted to be. God's way is the way to life, always!

Last week we talked about Deuteronomy, the second telling of the law that Moses gave to the generation that would inherit the promised land.

READ DEUTERONOMY 32:45-47 and notice how Moses ended his big speech.

How did Moses describe God's words in these verses?

What promise from God was connected to their obedience to His words?

Even though Moses warned them, God's people forgot God as the years went by. They were full from the blessings of the promised land, and it numbed them to see what truly made their home wonderful: the God who gave the blessings. Even in "perfect" homes, sin has a way of sneaking in.

READ DEUTERONOMY 8:11-20.

Why do you think we're prone to forget God when life is full?

How can you enjoy God's blessings without forgetting "every good and perfect gift is from above, coming down from the Father of lights" (James 1:17)?

And so, eventually, God left. He removed the special expression of His presence from the temple. As it turns out, home was more than a place, more than people, more than peace—it was a Person. God was training His people to want Him, not just what He could give them. After all, the whole point of this story of home is for God and His people to be together.

Why do you think we're prone to want God's promises without God's presence? How has that shown up in your life?

Of course, even though God's presence left the temple, He was still I AM. Because of this, there is good news ahead.

LOOK UP JOHN 17:24, **and write below what Jesus prayed.**

DAY TWO
LAMENTING WITH PSALM 137

Today, we're going to look at a psalm that's famously unquotable. The CSB calls Psalm 137 "Lament of the Exiles." Laments help people express the upsetting parts of themselves in prayer to God, and many laments include a bit of hope—but not this one.

In this psalm, the writer was reflecting on a time when he was homesick, grieving, and angry. It's a bit of an uncomfortable passage, so we're tempted to ignore it. But all of God's Word is good for us and equips us (2 Tim. 3:6-7)—and maybe this passage will help you navigate some uncomfortable parts of your story.

READ PSALM 137:1-4. **Where were the exiles?**

Why were they weeping? (Note: "Zion" represents their homeland, both the land and the temple.)

A "lyre" is a stringed instrument that was often used to accompany songs of praise and celebration,[4] but obviously this was not a time of celebration. It was cruel for the tormentors to ask them to sing!

READ VERSES 5-6.

God's people were in exile, away from Jerusalem, the city that represented the Lord, because they had *not* remembered God and His words. How might Psalm 137:5-6 be words of repentance?

The Edomites were neighbors to God's people and descendants of Esau, Jacob's brother (Gen. 25:30; 36:9). When enemies came to conquer Jerusalem, this "brother nation" cheered.

Has someone ever seen you in pain and cheered? If so, how did that feel?

The psalmist wanted God to remember this specific pain. The Hebrew word "remember" implies action.[5] The psalmist wanted God to *see* and *do* something about this injustice.

This part may feel "ungodly," but the psalmist wasn't taking vengeance into his own hands—his cry was "Remember, LORD!" God is I AM, so of course He sees and will always deal with sin. Pastor and podcaster Paul Carter puts it like this: "In the end, no one gets away with anything. All sins will be paid for in blood. Either the blood of Christ or the blood of sinners. It is not wrong to long for the justice of God."[6] God *remembers* the painful parts of our stories.

Is there an event in your "story of home" where you need to trust God to remember? If so, write your own version of verse 7 in the space below.

Even though we understand that the psalmist is looking to God for justice rather than taking it into his own hands, there are two sticky places we need to look at.

1. The word "happy" or "blessed." Eek!

The Hebrew word *esher* used here and typically translated *blessed* is taken from the root word *ashar*, which means "to go straight, go on, advance." So "blessedness" or "happiness" is not a flippant or light "happy birthday" but something more substantial that stems from doing the right thing. Scholar J. Alec Motyer translated the word like this in verse 9: "How *right* he will be who seizes and shatters your children against a rock!"[7] The psalmist believes it will be just, right, fair, and blessed if God repays Babylon with "what you have done to us" (v. 8). That brings us to the second bit of sticky business.

2. The dashing of babies on rocks. Double eek. Triple eek. All the eeks!

We are right to be shocked by this. It makes sense that this passage is famously avoided. But when we pay close attention to verse 8 "happy is the one who pays you back what you have done to us," we realize that verse 9 reveals what Babylon had already done to the exiles. Babylon had dashed *their* children against the rocks. The psalmist was not inventing a dark punishment for his oppressors; he was preserving a horrific, traumatic memory. He was asking God to give them justice for what had been brutally done to them.

How does it change your understanding of the psalm to realize the psalmist is recalling something that had already happened?

Psalm 137 is the honest prayer of a person who had been profoundly mistreated. Maybe you relate to that! You don't have to "delete" your anger or hate, pretend your experience wasn't real, or play the bubbly Christian girl. Smiling isn't your savior! In fact, that kind of response isn't even biblical. But it *is* biblical for us to use God's Word to help us engage with what is going on and to look to our true Savior. God's Word helps us navigate our stories and to view them in light of the truest, biggest story of home. After all, this psalm points us to Jesus:

- God the Father allowed His Son—His little one—to be dashed.[8]

- God the Son willingly hung on a tree, like those lyres, as many of His followers sat down and wept.[9]

- The exiles were mocked by their tormentors, and Jesus was, too. "He saved others; let him save himself" (Luke 23:35-39).

Why did Jesus endure all of that? To make the way for sinners to come home. To make the way for you to be with Him. Sin will not win in your story—Jesus wins!

Of course, even when we remember that, our lives aren't all shiny and perfect—not yet. Psalm 137 is a difficult lament, designed to help God's people through difficult times. As Eugene Peterson said, "We put on our 'Sunday best' in our prayers. But when we pray the prayers of God's people, the psalms, we find that will not do. We must pray who we actually are, not who we think we should be."[10] He sees you right where you are, and He's promised to bring you home.

If you need to, spend some time in honest prayer with God.

DAY THREE
PRAYING GOD'S PROMISES

During the exile, Daniel was a man who kept his eyes toward home and Homemaker, despite how Babylonian leaders sought to strip him of his heritage. He's a powerful example of faithfulness to God in a foreign land. While he was estranged, he was willing to be strange. He prayed on a regular basis, obeyed God's laws, and read God's Word.

LOOK UP JEREMIAH 25:11-13 AND JEREMIAH 29:10 to see some of what Daniel read. What do these two passages say about the exile?

When Daniel realized the exile had an expiration date that was quickly approaching, he responded in a very Daniel way. He prayed.

READ DANIEL 9:1-19.

Describe Daniel's posture as he prayed (vv. 3-4).

According to Daniel, why were the exiles in exile (vv. 5-6)?

According to Daniel, why should God deliver them (vv. 17-19)?

How can you tell that Daniel desired God's presence and not merely stuff or events God had promised?

Daniel was saturated with God's Word! In this text, he referenced both Jeremiah and Moses. In mentioning Moses, Daniel was speaking of the first five books of the Old Testament. He also listed characteristics of God over and over again. This was a man who truly sought to know God as He has revealed Himself in His Word. As a result, Daniel also had a clear and accurate understanding of his people and their sin. (When we look at God, it's easier to see our sin.)

Sometimes when we want someone to get over something we've done, we act like it wasn't that bad. Daniel did the exact opposite. He was brutally honest about the shortcomings of his people and appealed to God's character. In other words, Daniel wasn't saying, "What we've done isn't that bad." He was saying, "Who You are is so good!"

What do you learn from Daniel's prayer that should shape your prayer life?

Sometimes we feel like we "should" read God's Word and pray, but how might Daniel's example create a genuine desire to do those things?

As soon as Daniel started praying, God sent His angel Gabriel with an answer. Gabriel said he came because Daniel was "treasured by God" (v. 23). Then, Gabriel shared a mysterious prophecy with all kinds of numbers, mainly sevens (vv. 24-27), which represented fullness or completeness in ancient near eastern and Israelite culture.[11] Daniel had been amazed by God's promise to Jeremiah to complete the exile in seven decades, but as David Guzik says, "It was as if God said through Gabriel, 'Now I will show you some "sevens" that will really amaze you.'"[12]

The seventy years promised through Jeremiah was just the start of the waiting. They'd go home, but it wouldn't truly feel like home. (The books of Ezra and Nehemiah give evidence that this was true.) Sin was the true enemy that needed to be dealt with—not the Babylonians. But, in the fullness of time, a truer home would be revealed through the coming of the "Anointed One" (v. 25). The Greek word *Christ* and the Hebrew word *Messiah* both mean "Anointed One." Most commentators believe in one way or another, this mysterious prophecy points to Jesus!

Write Galatians 4:4-5 below, and circle the part about completion/fullness of time.

God the Father would send God the Son to make the way home by defeating the enemy of sin and making a way for God and people to be together. This is a much better promise of home than return from exile. Jesus is the only One who would be able to fulfill the exile promise: *"I will give you new hearts, and I will bring you home."*

DAY FOUR
WHERE ARE YOU?

The exile reminds us that mistreatment, betrayal, anger, hate, and horror might feel like unwanted, unfair, and unexpected plot twists in our stories of home—but these actions and emotions are the result when sin is wreaking havoc.

Whether you have endured these things because of your own sin, because of the direct sin of another, or because you simply live in a world impacted by sin, you can know that God the Father remembers what you've endured (meaning He sees and will act!) and God the Son understands what you've endured.

I want to share with you a letter from a fellow sister in Christ. And actually, this week's letter is from me! Thanks for letting me share some of my story. I hope it'll point you to God's story of home and help you feel less alone in your story.

Dear Sister,

As a kid, church always felt like an extension of home for me. I loved the music, taking notes during the sermon (okay, passing notes too), and seeing how many Bibles I could hand to my dad while he was distracted in lobby conversations before he noticed his daughter was a menace to society. (I think my record was six?) My family often went to lunch with my grandparents after church, where we could count on Dad and Granddad arguing over the bill because they both wanted to pay. Meanwhile, my siblings and I ate JELL-O. It was a good time.

When I went to college, I noticed that homesickness was especially pinchy on Sundays. My then boyfriend and now husband, Luke, once drove a sad Caroline six hours home on a Sunday afternoon and back the next day. He didn't mind at all. He's a good dude.

Luke and I got married right out of college, and he became a pastor. I assumed church and Sundays would continue to be a favorite part of my week. Maybe that's why the betrayal shocked me so badly.

We were part of a church that felt like family. We felt loved; we felt like we belonged—until influential people in the church decided we were enemies. It was startling, nauseating, disorienting. Though there were public smiles, behind closed doors some people rooted for and plotted our exit. Suddenly, there were whispers about us everywhere.

We had to move, leaving behind our first house and our precious community. I remember sitting in my daughter's nursery, overcome with affection for this precious room and all the memories it held, weeping as I peeled off the gold polka dots that I'd so happily placed on the walls in anticipation of her arrival. How had our beloved home been taken from us so quickly? I was sad, angry, and confused.

It wasn't really exile, but it felt like exile. Even still, the painful season held some of my most treasured memories, like when a friend assured me, "We are friends no matter what!" Or when another friend called and said, "I know the real you. I am with you." I still cry when I think about these friends. They were home to me when everything felt unsettled. Thank You, God!

It's not how I would have written the story, but now that we're years down the road, I'm grateful for the twists and turns. It felt like the floor was pulled out from under us, but that's where I learned God was my foundation. It felt like a home had been lost, but that's where I learned about the home God has promised me.

Our stories are a mix of glorious and gory moments, but I really do believe it all points us to God's promises. They are real, and I'm grateful for any reminder of that. Hang in there, sister.

With love,

— CAROLINE SAUNDERS

Use the space below (or your own journal) to respond to this letter. You may want to use the following questions to guide your response.

What thoughts and feelings are you experiencing as you consider my story?

What from the letter most resonates with you and why?

How does my story help you remember God's invitation to belong and be loved?

AWAY FROM HOME

Deaf to the sirens,
The words of the prophets,
God's people were captured
Just as He promised

Their home was destroyed
Homesickness their story
They'd welcomed sin,
They'd exchanged glory

Exile brought pain
Separation from God the worst
If God promised blessings
Why did they feel cursed?

Lament was their song
Weeping their standard
But with eyes on God
They endured the slander

Praying with eyes toward home
God's character in mind
They knew He was I AM
In every place and time

Even away from home
They remained in God's view
He wouldn't delete the bad
But He would bring them through

They'd remake their home
But the very best part
Was the God-made change
He'd remake their hearts

Even away from home
God's mercies were new
God never changes
His promises still true

The
WAY
HOME

session five

"Lord," Thomas said,
"we don't know where you're going.
How can we know the way?"
Jesus told him, "I am the way . . . "

JOHN 14:5-6A

God's people finally returned home, but even this wasn't the great homecoming they'd envisioned. Something wasn't quite right. The prophet Ezekiel had told God's people they needed new hearts—hearts that could and would follow God. But how could that happen? Things seemed bleak and beige, but all the while God was carrying out His plan. At just the right time, God the Father said to His Son, "It's time to build the way home." God Himself came to dwell on earth as a baby. As He grew, He pointed people to the way. The way wasn't a path: it was a Person. It was Him. Jesus is the answer to every promise of home that God has spoken along the way, and through Him, all are invited: "Come home."

GROUP GUIDE

session five

COME ON IN

God's people came back home, but life in the promised land wasn't as glorious as it was in the golden era of King Solomon. The new temple couldn't compare to the original (Hag. 2:3), and no prophets spoke words from God. The land itself seemed like it could slip away. Everything—including God's promises—felt fragile.

Have you ever been through a time when it felt like God was silent? Explain.

REMEMBER, MESSIAH, OR CHRIST, MEANS "ANOINTED ONE."

They thought they'd arrived home, but God's people were waiting for home to arrive. The Hebrew Scriptures make it clear that they were no longer waiting for a place but for a Person—the Messiah. They kept watch, and they wondered why God seemed to be silent. But God hadn't abandoned His people. He was building the way home.

Let's begin building with Matthew 1. This is a genealogy (a list of family generations). Interestingly, genealogy means "genesis"—a beginning.[1] Just as the Old Testament began with a home being made, the New Testament does too! Rather than list every single generation, Matthew shaped this genealogy into neat categories to show us God's careful design in "building" the house:

- Matthew traces the lineage fourteen generations from Abraham to King David (vv. 2-6).

- He traces a second fourteen, King David to the time of the Babylonian exile (vv. 7-11).

- He traces a third fourteen, going fourteen generations forward from the exile (vv. 12-16).

IT'S OKAY IF YOU STRUGGLE WITH PRONUNCIATION OR DON'T RECOGNIZE THESE PEOPLE. THAT'S PART OF THE POINT!

READ VERSES 12-16 OUT LOUD. What names do you recognize in verse 16?

Through this genealogy, Matthew was saying, "Look at what God has been building! This is the One you've been waiting for!"

I want you to be a girl who clings to God's promises—especially when God seems silent and life makes no sense. God's promises aren't fragile collectibles we stick on a high shelf because we're afraid to break them. They're like the stuffed animal that we sleep with every night and secretly bring to every sleepover. So, let's take a moment to remember the promises we've collected so far:

- ☐ **In Session 1, we talked about the first home, Eden. The Eden promise is,** *"The enemy of home will be destroyed."*

- ☐ **In Session 2, we talked about Abraham, Isaac, and Jacob. The Abrahamic promises are,** *"I will give you a place, and I will make you a people who can both enjoy and pass along my blessing,"* **and,** *"Wherever you are, I will be with you."*

- ☐ **In Session 3, we talked about the time of Moses and the tabernacle through the time of Solomon and the temple. The Moses, tabernacle, and temple promises are these:** *"I want to be with you. I will lead you home. Home is where I AM is."*

- ☐ **In Session 4, we talked about exile. This terrible experience highlighted all the previous promises:** *The enemy of home will be destroyed—even if it lives in your own hearts. Repent! Only I can give you a place and make you a people who can both enjoy and pass along my blessing. Repent! I want to be with you. I will lead you home, so look to me. Home is where I AM is. Repent!* **But to truly repent in a way that stuck, God's people would need new hearts. That's why the exile promise is,** *"I will give you new hearts, and I will bring you home."*

Today, we will look at how Jesus is the fulfillment of all of the promises we've encountered so far—and therefore the way home. When you see He's fulfilled a promise, **come back to this list, and check it off.** I'm excited to make these connections with you!

TAKE A SEAT

READ JOHN 1:1-13.

How does John describe Jesus in verse 1?

Think back to Genesis 1–2. How did God create the world?

Where was Jesus during creation (John 1:2)? What do you think it means that "all things were created *through* [Jesus]," (v. 3, emphasis added)?

John reveals to His readers right away that Jesus wasn't just with I AM at the beginning, Jesus *is* I AM. That means Jesus is all that Exodus 34 stuff: compassionate and gracious, slow to anger and abounding in steadfast love. All of those qualities of God Himself had come near in a new way through God the Son!

How does John describe Jesus in verse 4?

Back at the beginning, I AM placed limits on the light and darkness. But what can this light (Jesus) do (Gen. 1:5)?

The religious leaders of Jesus's day thought they knew God. How did they respond to Jesus? What does this tell you about their relationship with God?

What does Jesus give to people who do receive Him (John 1:12)?

Those who receive this Word, Jesus, in faith are given the right to become children of God. This Word is the way to family.

Think back to Abraham. God promised Abraham he would be the father of a multitude, and through his family, the whole world would be blessed. Through Abraham's descendant Jesus, we become a family of faith. We come under Jesus's blessing, and we pass it along to the world. (Hold off on your checking—there's more to come on the Abrahamic promises!)

Write John 1:14 below.

The word *dwelt* can be literally translated "tabernacled." Commentators believe John used this word purposefully, so that we'd connect back to that old tabernacle.[2] It always pointed to Jesus, the way home.

The temple pointed to Jesus, too! If you've read about Jesus's baptism, you might remember that the sky opened up, God the Father spoke, and the Holy Spirit descended on Jesus. It reminds us of the way God's glory descended on the temple. Jesus's baptism was the installment of the true temple. Ezekiel saw God's glory leave the old temple, but it returned within a Person.

Jesus is the answer to the Moses, tabernacle, and temple promises: *"I want to be with you. I will lead you home. Home is where I AM is."* **Go ahead and check it off!**

Of course, for Jesus to make the way home, there was an enemy to conquer: sin. Throughout the story, we've seen that sin is a big deal to God. He forgives it, and He punishes it (Ex. 34:6-7). It's hard to figure out how that works until we get to Jesus. God is able to forgive because Jesus endured the punishment. When your sin is forgiven, it's not like it fell in the universe's couch cushions and got lost: it was placed on Jesus.

Write 2 Corinthians 5:21 below.

We typically think of death as a defeat, but Jesus's death was a victory. Why? Because it knocked the weapons of sin and shame out of Satan's hands (Col. 2:15). No longer could Satan accuse us of our guilt. Anyone who looks to Jesus is no longer guilty. That person is more than innocent—that person is righteous! He or she is welcomed home, embraced, and celebrated. That person will belong and be loved forever. Jesus is the answer to the Eden promise: *"The enemy of home will be destroyed."* **Go ahead and check it off!**

Jesus was crucified alongside two other men—criminals who were being punished for their crimes, their guilt and shame on display for all to see. And yet, in this hopeless place, one of these sinners found the way home.

READ LUKE 23:39-43, and write verse 43 below.

Notice the two ways Jesus described home in verse 43: "with me" and "paradise." Home is where I AM is!

A criminal turned into a child of God through a heart made new. A dying, hopeless man found the way home by looking to Jesus. Jesus is the answer to the exile promise: *"I will give you new hearts, and I will bring you home."* **Go ahead and check it off!**

Jesus and this man died, but that isn't the end of the story. Death is a dark reality in a sin-soaked world, but remember what John said about Jesus: "The light shines in the darkness, and yet the darkness did not overcome it" (John 1:5). Jesus conquered death!

Jesus hinted at this before He died, but people didn't get it. When He flipped over tables in the temple, people asked, "What reason do you have for doing this?" Jesus said, "Destroy this temple, and I will raise it up in three days" (John 2:19). He wasn't talking about the temple building: He was talking about His temple body. They would destroy it, but God Himself would rebuild it, and this glorious rebuilding would shift the history of the world. Jesus stepped out of the tomb in a resurrected body, and His followers stood in awe.

LOOK UP MATTHEW 28:19-20 to see some of the resurrected Jesus's last words before He ascended to heaven.

What did Jesus say His followers should do? Where could they go?

As they went, where would Jesus be?

Jesus is the fulfillment of another part of the Abrahamic promises: *"Wherever you are, I will be with you."* And if you're keeping track, there's one more aspect to the Abrahamic promises—a place. When Jesus taught His famous Sermon on the Mount,

He said, "Blessed are the humble, for they will inherit the earth" (Matt. 5:5). When I looked into the definition of the Greek word translated "inherit," I learned how closely it's linked with the word *possess*. In fact, it wouldn't be too far off to paraphrase the verse like this: *Blessed are the meek: for they shall possess the land.* God's children experience a measure of Jesus's blessing of home the moment they follow Him—but they also look ahead to the day they will be literally, physically home with God. The day they possess the land. More on that day coming soon!

For now, know this: Jesus is the answer to the Abrahamic promises. **Go ahead and check it off!** In fact, He's the fulfillment of all the promises we've collected along the way! He is the way home.

LET'S TALK

How does the genealogy in Matthew show us God was working out His plan the entire time?

When you look back over your life history and beyond, how do you see God at work?

How would you explain to someone who is not a Christian that Jesus is only the way home?

LET'S PRAY

Even when (especially when?) we aren't sure what God is doing, His promises are true. The best way to remember this is through Jesus. Second Corinthians 1:20 says, "For all of God's promises have been fulfilled in Christ with a resounding 'Yes!'" (NLT). Which of the home promises are you most craving in your life right now? This craving reveals where you desire more of Jesus. Spend some time praying for one another to experience more of Jesus in these specific places.

DAY ONE
JESUS'S STORY OF HOME

Hebrews 4:15 says, "For we do not have a high priest who is unable to sympathize with our weaknesses, but one who has been tempted in every way as we are, yet without sin." The word translated *sympathize* means "to be affected with the same feeling as another."[3] This verse is about Jesus, and it teaches us that Jesus understands the pains, joys, difficulties, and anxieties of your story of home—not just because He's God but because He's man and has experienced these things Himself.

Let's take a look at His earthly life:

BIRTH AND EARLY CHILDHOOD

Jesus's mother Mary gave birth away from their hometown of Nazareth. She and Joseph were in Bethlehem to be counted for a census. About 90 to 120 miles from home (depending on the route[4]), Mary and Joseph weren't able to secure lodging one could typically expect to find in first-century Palestine. So, Jesus was born in an environment that probably felt like the opposite of home—and soon became even more uncomfortable.

LOOK UP MATTHEW 2:13-23.

What part of this text . . .

. . . reminds you of Moses's story as a baby?

. . . reminds you of the Israelites' deliverance from Pharaoh?

. . . reminds you of the exile?

How might the memory of the announcement about Jesus's birth have been a comfort to Mary and Joseph during this scary season (Luke 1:30-33)?

ADOLESCENCE

READ LUKE 2:41-52.

On their way home from the Passover festival in Jerusalem, Joseph and Mary realized Jesus wasn't in their traveling group. They went back and found Him conversing with the teachers in the temple. This passage contains the first recorded words of Jesus.

What were His first words, and why were they significant?

In this culture, it was normal for a son to take up his father's line of work, and since Jesus was twelve, He was near the time when sons began to be viewed as adults. Likely, young Jesus was growing in His understanding of His relationship with God the Father and the ultimate work set before Him. But at this point, the time of His ministry was still years away. So, He went home with Mary and Joseph, was obedient to them, and grew in every way (Luke 2:51-52).

ADULTHOOD

Throughout Jesus's ministry, we see Him stay in the homes of others, but He didn't have a home of His own. When He wanted to retreat from the world (and He often did!), He would slip away to a quiet, outdoor place and pray.

LOOK UP LUKE 9:57-58.

What did Jesus say about His home in this passage?

READ MARK 3:21 AND JOHN 7:5.

Our families have such an impact on our stories of home. What family tension do you see here?

The Gospels only give us a few glimmers of Jesus's early life, but Hebrews 4:15 can give you confidence that Jesus understands any painful home experience you've endured. You don't have an unbothered Savior—but One who has been willingly affected. In Jesus, there's both triumph and in-the-trenches tenderness. You are not alone!

Use the space below to write a prayer both thanking Jesus for understanding you and asking Him to help you more deeply experience the blessing of being understood by Him.

DAY TWO
JESUS AND GLORY

Have you ever heard Jesus called "Immanuel, God with us"? It's a pretty powerful idea. After all, a huge theme in God's story is God dwelling with man. In the beginning, there was perfect "with-ness" in the garden, but after sin entered the picture, God provided other ways for with-ness. Today we'll examine "God with us" by looking at the tabernacle, the temple, the exile—and how they all point to Jesus, who is Immanuel, God with us.

TABERNACLE

LOOK UP EXODUS 40:34-38.

What covered the tabernacle?

What happened to Moses?

According to this text, did the Israelites know the way to the promised land?

In the wilderness, God's glory "filled the tabernacle" (v. 34), then settled—or dwelled—there (v. 35). The Israelites based their migration to the promised land on the movement of God. When He moved, they moved. Wherever they went, God was with them.

What covered the temple?

What happened to the priests?

According to Solomon, how long would God dwell with them in this way?

In the promised land, God's glory filled the temple (v. 11), then settled—or dwelled— there (v. 13). The people of God were home, and God was with them. The tabernacle pointed ahead to this. However, this "with-ness" was limited by a veil (or curtain) that separated the holy of holies (the place where God's presence was said to abide) from the rest of the temple. Because of the seriousness of sin and the holiness of God, no one could come behind this veil, with one exception: the high priest, once a year on the Day of Atonement (Ex. 26:33–35; Lev. 16:2).

EXILE

Unfortunately, God's people "exchanged their Glory for useless idols" (Jer. 2:11b) and did not care about holiness or sin (Ezek. 22:26). During the exile, Ezekiel had a vision of God's presence leaving the temple (Ezek. 10). God was still I AM, but He removed the special expression of His presence from the sacred place. To have true home, to have glorious with-ness, God needed to provide a temple that could not be defiled, that could atone for the sins of the people, and could make a way for them to be holy.

JESUS

LOOK UP MATTHEW 3:13-17. **What in this text reminds you of the other texts we've read today?**

Similar to God's glory coming to rest on and dwell in the tabernacle and the temple, God's Spirit came to rest on Jesus! This happened at the very beginning of Jesus's ministry and was essentially the dedication of the new and true temple.

Interestingly, when Jesus died on the cross, the veil separating the holy of holies from the rest of the temple was ripped from top to bottom (Matt. 27:45-51). The sacrificial death of Jesus, the true temple, did two important things for anyone who looks to Jesus: it dealt with our sin, and it made us holy! Christ made a way for anyone to access God through Him. The ripped curtain became an invitation: "Come home."

LOOK UP JOHN 17:24 **and write it below.**

Jesus promised that even after He ascended to heaven, He wouldn't leave His followers alone. God would still be with them in an even closer way than before. Jesus would send God the Spirit to live in His followers (John 14:16-17)!

Yes, there will certainly be times when we feel alone. But here's something truer than that feeling: God is with us.

DAY THREE
THE WAY

When we follow Jesus, our feet are placed solidly and permanently on the journey home. But following Jesus doesn't mean we experience a perfect home here and now. We still experience a measure of separation that can be deeply painful in a number of ways, but we find comfort and strength in Jesus's promises of home.

READ JOHN 14:1-7.

Jesus spoke these comforting words to His disciples the night before His violent departure from them. The beautiful togetherness Jesus's disciples enjoyed with Him was about to be severed—first through betrayal, then through abandonment, then through ridicule and torment, and finally through death on a cross. Jesus endured the full experience of separation, but His disciples experienced a measure of it, too.

> **What promises did Jesus offer to keep the hearts of the disciples from being troubled?**

> **Thomas said he didn't know the way, but he knew the Way (Jesus). In your own words, describe the difference.**

> **How might Jesus's promises and proclamation have encouraged His disciples during His death and even after His returned to heaven (v. 6)?**

Let's press John 14:1-7 into the fabric of our own experiences.

Consider your current circumstances. You may not know the way, but you know the Way. Why is this a crucial comfort for the confusing zigs and zags of life? How does this encourage you right now?

Consider your anxieties about the future. How does knowing that Jesus is preparing a place for you and will return make a difference on your journey?

All Christ followers experience "homesick" moments as we await Jesus's return—like loneliness or a longing for safety, peace, love, and joy. We long to be with God fully in a place where the enemy cannot enter and where with-ness can flourish.

When do you most feel spiritually homesick? Why?

Let me offer you a bit of wording that has been a comfort to me during my "homesick" moments—those moments when I feel lonely, confused, overwhelmed, or exhausted by the impact of sin in my life and on the world. It's two phrases: "Christ in" and "in Christ."

CHRIST IN

LOOK UP THESE VERSES: ROMANS 8:10; 2 CORINTHIANS 13:5; AND GALATIANS 2:20.

Based on these verses, what do you think "Christ in" means?

How can the reality of "Christ in" help you remember your true home in homesick moments?

IN CHRIST

LOOK UP THESE VERSES: ROMANS 8:1; 2 CORINTHIANS 5:17; AND GALATIANS 3:26.

Based on these verses, what do you think "in Christ" means?

How is the reality of being in Christ a "deposit of home" that can help you remember your true home in homesick moments?

If you follow Jesus, Christ dwells in you through God the Spirit. He is with you always. You are never alone, never forsaken.

If you follow Jesus, you are in Christ. When God looks at you, He sees Jesus. He looks at you as His true child. You are never unloved, never despised, never unwanted. You always belong.

Sister, if you are a Jesus follower, Christ is in you and you are in Christ. You may not know the way, but you know the Way—Jesus! May these truths wrap around you like a blanket and warm you from within like a cup of coffee. It's all true: a precious deposit of home belongs to you, your true home is being prepared with you in mind, and Jesus will return so that you can be with Him. Thank You, God!

DAY FOUR
A SISTER'S STORY OF HOME

Jesus's ministry is deeply personal to us. He endured the pains of human life and understands our stories of home. He conquered sin, the enemy that threatens our homes. He made the way for us to be with God—and in fact, He is the Way. It's a crucial comfort for the zigs and zags we experience on our journey home.

I want to share with you a letter from a fellow sister in Christ. As she shares her story of home, I hope it'll point you to God's story of home and help you feel less alone in your story.

Dear Friend,

Have you ever experienced a deep longing for such a lengthy time that it feels like an old friend? The desire to belong has been that for me. I've dealt with it for a good while, but most acutely since getting married and moving to the United States.

You see, I am a half-Palestinian Dominican who became an American citizen through marriage and am now serving Christ in the Middle East. For most of my life I'd taken for granted what it felt like to belong. "Better together" had been a way of life for my community in the Dominican Republic. But on my wedding day I tearfully hugged my people goodbye and moved to a new city in the States.

My husband and I loved opening our home for hospitality. But at first, I couldn't quite tell who wanted us to be their people (mostly because I misread cultural cues). Just as I felt like it was starting to happen, we moved to a very international city in the Middle East. I didn't realize though that I had unresolved grief and patterns of seeking refuge in people as a way of coping with it.

Our time in that city would be relatively short due to my husband's work, so I jumped into trying to do life with God's people there. But many factors made doing life in community very challenging and my longing to belong was not met in church relationships the way I hoped. This revealed sinful patterns I had developed.

When the time came to say goodbye, the Lord pierced my soul through His Word:

"I, I am he who comforts you;
who are you that you are afraid of man who dies. . . .
I am the LORD your God . . . [who says] to Zion, 'You are my people'"
(Isa. 51:12-16, ESV).

When I read the phrase, "You are my people," I burst out crying. I had been longing for years to hear other people say: "You guys are our people." But now here was the eternal God, establishing Himself as my place of belonging, and telling me, "Aylin, you are my people!"

Being in Christ reassures me that the things that matter to me matter deeply to God because He is my Father. He sees my desert spaces and comforts me. He makes my wilderness flourish like Eden (Isa. 51:3). His delight in being close to His people never stops. He even rides the heavens to come near and rescue (Deut. 33:26)! He loves knowing us, hearing from us, and talking with us. The Spirit shines His light where we struggle to believe because He wants us to be filled with the hope of knowing His intimate love (Rom. 5:2). Sister, do you see how the Triune God is our tribe as we go through the changes of life?

I have moved cross-culturally twice more since that day the Lord spoke to me. With each move, my Father keeps peeling back the layers of my story, sinking in more deeply what it means to know Him as home. I am sure He is doing the same with you, my friend. I am thankful He doesn't stop preparing us this side of eternity for our life together with Christ, our bridegroom. 'Til then, may His grace enable us to hear Him sing,
    "You are Mine, and I am yours."

— AYLIN MERCK, writer, Middle East

Use the space below (or your own journal) to respond to this letter. You may want to use the following questions to guide your response.

What thoughts and feelings are you experiencing as you consider this sister's story?

What from her letter most resonates with you and why?

How does her story help you remember God's invitation to belong and be loved?

THE WAY HOME

At the darkest moment
In the fullness of time
God sent the Way
To redeem all mankind

God came as a child
God came with a cry
God came without home
God came to die

He was the promised seed
Who came under Eden's sword
He was the true tabernacle
The God-with-us Lord

He was the true Temple
Upon Him was glory
The Way Home
Hope for exile's story

He lived the perfect life
The good news He proclaimed
Following the Father's will,
He took on our shame

He faced our great enemy
The sin that intruded
Into every human heart
Could now be uprooted

His tomb seemed the end
Sealed with a stone
But it could not hold Him
It wasn't His Home

We, the cursed,
Through Him are blessed
Our shame is gone
In His righteousness dressed

The darkness of sin
Has been overcome
By Jesus, the light
Who says to us, "Come!"

Almost
HOME

session six

In him you are also being built together for God's dwelling in the Spirit.

PAUL, EPHESIANS 2:22

Look, God's dwelling is with humanity, and he will live with them.

A LOUD VOICE FROM THE THRONE, REVELATION 21:3

Jesus didn't just fulfill promises; He made them. Before He returned to heaven, Jesus promised He would send a Helper (the Holy Spirit), and He promised He would return. These two promises are like fuel the rest of the Bible runs on—and fuel that allows Christians ever since the time of Jesus (including us!) to keep going. God Himself dwells in us, making us the new temple. Because of Jesus, we have access to God no matter where we are, no matter when we call, and no matter what we need. And though we still endure the challenges of a world saturated with sin, we look ahead to the day Jesus will return and finally make everything new and wonderful forever. Sister, we are almost home.

GROUP GUIDE

session six

COME ON IN

READ JOHN 14:16-18. **What did Jesus promise in verses 16-17?**

What did Jesus promise in verse 18?

Let's focus on that first promise, the Holy Spirit, for a bit.

After Jesus died and rose again, He returned to heaven. That's where He is right this moment, ruling in power! This has always been a comfort for Jesus's followers, because the moment a Christian dies, his or her soul immediately joins Jesus there, just as He taught the criminal on the cross who cried out to Him in faith.

But what about before death? Is it just, "Have fun down there, guys. I'll see ya when you're in heaven?" No way. We get a "deposit" of our true home (2 Cor. 5:5) and to experience togetherness with God through the Holy Spirit!

READ JOHN 14:26. **How did Jesus describe the Holy Spirit?**

What did Jesus say the Holy Spirit would do?

READ JOHN 14:23 **and write it below.**

If we're not reading carefully, we can assume this verse means something like, "If you love me, you better act right, and then I'll hang out with you." But that's not at all what Jesus is saying. If you remember from our study of the exile, part of the promise of home is that God will remake hearts (Ezek. 36:26-28). He'd give His people a new Spirit—His Spirit—to help them follow Him and defeat the enemy of home.

TAKE A SEAT

The promise of the Holy Spirit was fulfilled during Pentecost, the Jewish harvest festival was also called "the Feast of Weeks" because it happened about seven weeks after Passover. (So, it would have been nearly fifty days after Jesus's death and resurrection, and approximately ten days after Jesus's ascension to heaven.) Because of the exile centuries before, Jewish people lived all over the world, and many traveled to the temple in Jerusalem for this festival. But, on this Pentecost, they ended up encountering an unexpected and new temple.

READ ACTS 2:2-11.

How does verse 2 remind you of the way God's glory descended on the tabernacle, the temple, and on Jesus?

What did the people hear (v. 6,11)?

From what we know of God's story, it looks like a new temple is being made—this time within the bodies of Jesus's followers! By the power of the Holy Spirit, Peter began to preach a sermon that gripped the hearts of those who listened.

READ VERSES 37-41.

What did Peter tell the crowd to do?

Who did Peter say God's promise of the Holy Spirit was for?

How many people were added to their number that day?

This isn't just a cool day at church—this is the birthday of the church! We can assume that many of the Jews present traveled back to their homes, carrying with them the promise of the truer home. The temple building had been a "come and see" kind of home, but this new temple, temple bodies, was a "go and tell" kind of home. This home became Jesus's invitation to the world: "Come home."

And this home was just as thoughtfully built and glorious (if not more so) as the tabernacle and the temple. Notice two "opposites" about this temple that are totally true:

PETER'S NAME WAS GIVEN TO HIM BY JESUS, AND IT MEANS "ROCK." FROM THE BEGINNING, PETER WAS TOLD THAT HE WAS A PART OF THIS NEW TEMPLE BUILDING, THE CHURCH.

- This new temple is an *individual* thing. Jesus said He and the Father would come make their home in the one who loves Him (John 14:23). He promised us the Holy Spirit who would live in each of us, which we see happen on Pentecost to individual believers and which we see happen to individual believers throughout the book of Acts. (Look up 1 Cor. 6:19-20 for more on this idea.)

- This new temple is a *group* thing. In ancient construction, the first stone put in place was called the cornerstone. The rest of the work was built on this foundational element.[1] Peter described Jesus as the cornerstone upon which the church is built and said Christians are "living stones" that are built into a spiritual house, the new temple (1 Pet. 2:4-5).

God has always been an incredible builder and artist—and this is especially evident in the church.

READ EPHESIANS 2:19-22. In your own words, describe this "home" of people.

You might have heard that the church isn't a building, it's people. That idea comes from passages like this. Because the Holy Spirit lives in God's people now, the people together are God's temple.

Of course, there's still that enemy to consider—sin. Because of Jesus's work on the cross, the sin is paid, and God will never leave these new temple bodies. But sin is a wedge. (Think about the way sin can keep you from feeling close to someone you live with.) It gets in the way of our experience of togetherness with God and one another, and it gets in the way of our "go and tell" calling. The New Testament letters often warn churches against sin that happens within us and sin that happens between us. We need to guard against both by the power of the Holy Spirit.

> **What do you think guarding against sin looks like for _individual_ people?**

In 1 Corinthians 6:19, we find that the body of a Christian is a temple. Some assume this means physical stuff, like nutrition and exercise. Of course, those things can be done to the glory of God, but have you ever noticed that they can also be done to the glory of self? That sometimes we want to sculpt our bodies in the same way that Old Testament people sculpted idols? Our enemy isn't cinnamon rolls—it's sin! Treating our bodies like temples is actually a call to walk with God rather than let sin make its home in our hearts.

> **What do you think guarding against sin looks like for _groups_ of people?**

Living as the temple isn't just about fighting the enemy—it's about loving our Father and our family. We celebrate one another's gifts, use our own gifts faithfully, and remember the wonderful ending of the story.

Throughout the study, we've seen the shape of God's promise of home the way we might see the shape of a present beneath its wrapping. But the final book of the Bible, Revelation (which means unveiling), gives us a glorious peek behind the wrapping paper through a vision that God gave to John the disciple. Jesus will return, and He'll make a new heaven and earth, establishing the homiest home where we can be fully, finally, and forever with Him!

READ REVELATION 21:1-5.

What is new? What is no more?

What part of this passage excites you the most?

Think on all the promises we've collected and how they sparkle:

1. The Eden promise is *"The enemy of home will be destroyed."* When Jesus returns, the serpent and sin will be fully, finally, forever destroyed. Even the sin that Christians still struggle with in our own hearts will be gone, and we will look like Jesus!

2. The Abrahamic promises are *"I will give you a place, and I will make you a people who can both enjoy and pass along my blessing,"* and *"Wherever you are, I will be with you."* When Jesus returns, heaven and earth will be made new, and the full family of those who have humbly looked to Him as Savior will possess, inherit, and find that they are home with Him, fully, finally, and forever.

3. The Moses, tabernacle, and temple promises are *"I want to be with you. I will lead you home,"* and *"Home is where I AM is."* The day Jesus returns, those promises will no longer be something we cling to in faith but something we see spectacularly and plainly on display all around us. The whole world will be a temple of togetherness (Hab. 2:14; Rev. 21:22).

4. The exile promise is *"I will give you new hearts, and I will bring you home."* Those who repent and look to Jesus in faith, no matter where they've been or what they've done, are dressed gloriously and invited to come in. God has brought the exiles home (Rev. 7:14; 22:14).

LOOK UP REVELATION 22:20, and write down these very important words that conclude this big story.

The title of this Bible study is an invitation to us from Jesus and our invitation to others: "Come home." But in a sense, it is also the cry of our hearts to Jesus: "Come, Lord Jesus!" We want to be home with Him! If you feel homesick, take heart. When Jesus returns, we will be home—finally, fully, and forever.

LET'S TALK

Is it a little strange to think about the Holy Spirit living inside you? How would you explain what that means to a kid or a new Christian?

We won't be perfect, but we can fight sin and grow in godliness by the power of the Holy Spirit. How has the Holy Spirit been a helper to you in the past few days and weeks?

As God's people, we are the "go and tell" temple. What does that mean and does that describe your church?

What are you currently doing to keep both the individual temple and the collective temple healthy and functioning for God's purpose and His glory?

LET'S PRAY

Share an area of your life where you need to remember that God is with you and Jesus will one day return and make everything new. Partner up and pray for one another.

DAY ONE
GOD'S POSTURE TOWARD THOSE WHO COME HOME

The word *home* gives warm fuzzy feelings of comfort, closeness, and belonging. So, we can sometimes feel a weird tension when we think about God's invitation to us to "come home" and the promised home we'll have with Him. After all, God is holy and perfect—how could sinners like us ever actually be home with Him? Won't we feel unwanted on some level? Won't we suspect that He's a little grossed out by our sinfulness? Won't He be disappointed in us?

Yes, the promises sound good. But are we truly loved by the Promise Keeper? Is God someone who does "good stuff" or is God good? And if God is good, will God be good to *me*?

Does this tension feel familiar to you? Explain.

The promises of home run deeper than God doing a thing. They are about God offering His very self to people who don't deserve His love—yet He gladly dumps it over our heads like those big buckets at a water park.

READ LUKE 15:11-32.

THE YOUNGER SON (VERSES 11-20a)

How did the younger son treat his father?

What foolish choices did the younger son make, and what were the consequences of those choices?

Pigs were considered unclean by Jewish people (Lev. 11:7), so caring for pigs and longing to eat their food was humiliating and shameful. But verse 17 is a huge turning point in the story. It says about the young man, "When he came to his senses" (CSB), or "But when he came to himself" (ESV).

What do you think this phrase means? Have you ever experienced something similar to this? Explain.

What did the son hope would happen when he returned home?

THE FATHER (VERSES 20b–24)

Normally, how would you expect a father who has been treated this way to respond to his son? How would you expect him to look (facial expression, posture, etc.)?

What does verse 20 tell you about the heart of the father toward his younger son?

The father's love for the son was greater than anything the son had done. He hoped to be allowed to be a servant, but he was joyfully celebrated as a son. The younger son represents anyone who has looked to Jesus in repentance. No matter what pigsty we've been sitting in, the Father moves toward us in love and welcomes us home!

THE OLDER SON (VERSES 25–32)

It's interesting that Jesus did not end the parable with the return of the son and the celebration that followed. He included another character in the story—the older son.

Why was the older son angry?

In what way does the older son's response reveal how scandalous the father's love was and that the older son was missing the point?

How do you see the heart of God in this parable?

Like the older son, we have a tendency to shift our focus from the Father's goodness to our own "goodness" (or shame, stuff, circumstances, etc.). Distracted, we forget the nature of the Father's love. The enemy whispers doubts, and we believe him. We think the Father will keep away from unclean sinners—but God moves toward us at our worst!

Christ's heart for sinners is clear on the pages of Scripture. Why does it sometimes get so muddled in our hearts?

LOOK UP REVELATION 21:3-4 and write it below.

This is a collective word for God's people because it is an individual word for each of God's children. You are loved and welcomed by God. His invitation to "come home" has your name on it. He doesn't reluctantly let you in—His eyes are full of delight, and His arms are wide open.

Write a prayer sharing with God any part of this that's hard to grasp—and rejoice over what is true!

DAY TWO
LIVING LIKE WE'RE HEADED HOME

Way back in Ezekiel 36:24-28, God promised He would send His Spirit. In our group time, we read Acts 2 and saw this moment come to pass. When we place our faith in Jesus, we are rescued from our sin and born into a forever family by the indwelling of the Holy Spirit.

The Holy Spirit unites us. He gives us a shared spiritual DNA with other believers. Those of us who share addresses, languages, and customs can't begin to pull off the kind of unity that God is creating!

The Holy Spirit also shapes us. God is transforming individuals who can and will follow Him fully—and can therefore be totally at home with Him. The gift of the Holy Spirit is kind of like God saying, "You're my kid! Now, let me parent you." He is raising us to look like Christ (Rom. 8:29) and to love one another—something we'll be able to do fully, finally, and forever when Jesus returns. We call this process sanctification—or as I like to call it, "holy growin.'"

Of course, growing is slow and clunky. Kids fall down when they're learning to walk, and they stumble over words when they're learning to talk. One of my kids ate a dead spider. (Cool.) Being a kid can be messy—so can being God's kid. We're not grown yet, and we're not home yet, but we're on our way.

God ultimately does the work of growing us both as individual Christians and as a part of the Christian family, but we participate with Him. We don't earn our place in God's family, but we do overflow it. God's love for us always impacts how we live!

READ 1 PETER 2:1-5.

What should we as Christians get rid of, and what should we desire?

PETER WROTE TO CHRISTIANS HE CALLED "EXILES" BECAUSE THEY, LIKE US, WERE WAITING FOR JESUS TO COME BACK, AND THEY WERE ENDURING PERSECUTION THAT LIKELY MADE THEM FEEL LIKE STRANGERS IN THEIR OWN CITIES. DURING THIS TIME IN HISTORY, CHRISTIANS WERE TREATED HORRIFICALLY BY LEADERS LIKE NERO, DOMITIAN, AND TRAJAN.[2] PETER WANTED THESE CHRISTIANS TO LIVE OUT THEIR FAITH NO MATTER WHAT.

Have you ever seen a newborn baby get very, very excited about a bottle of milk? Why do you think Peter is bringing that mental picture to mind?

Peter was calling us to crave the nutritious and delicious Word of God—the Bible! It's through the goodness of God's Word that we will grow up into Him. He referenced Psalm 34:8, which says, "Taste and see that the LORD is good." When we have experienced God's goodness, we'll want more. As we continue to taste His goodness through relationship with Him, we'll grow!

How have you experienced the goodness of God's Word?

What might numb your spiritual taste buds?

How did Peter describe Jesus in verse 4? How did he describe believers in verse 5?

READ VERSES 9-12.

How did Peter describe believers?

How is sin described in verse 11, and why should believers not live a sinful lifestyle?

Peter was counseling these believers to honor their true home by not letting sin make its home in their hearts. Since we are God's house, we need to let Him "rearrange the furniture" of our hearts any way He likes.

Do you sense God wanting to do any rearranging in your heart?

How do the truths found in 1 Peter 2:1-12 help you in your battle against sin?

Peter's words encourage us to examine our lives and to focus on who Jesus is, who we are because of Jesus, and our hope ahead. One day, we'll be fully grown as individual people and as a family—holy and united. Until then, we commit to growing with God by the power of the Holy Spirit.

DAY THREE
WHEN HEAVEN COMES HOME

Sometimes, we think of heaven as the place where goody-goody people go to play a harp while sitting on a cloud. It sounds a little boring—and, um, a little unbiblical. The clear information on heaven is limited, but we know one of the main promises of heaven: we will be with God (2 Cor. 5:8). At this point in this study, you're probably beginning to grasp that this is the deep craving of our souls.

But here's another promise: God will be with us. Randy Alcorn says, "When God's children die, we immediately go to heaven to be with Christ (Luke 23:43). But when we carefully read Scripture, we find that one day God will permanently relocate the present heaven to the newly transformed earth, which then will become the 'forever heaven.'"[3] Heaven itself isn't home yet.

The last three chapters of the Bible give us a sneak peek into this forever home, which Nancy Guthrie describes as "even better than Eden."[4] Since we know how awesome Eden was, that's pretty exciting!

Let's look at the "even better than Eden" home that awaits us by comparing the beginning with the end. Like most makeover shows, the Bible intentionally offers some incredible before and afters.

I KNOW THIS
SEEMS LIKE A LOT OF
FLIPPING, BUT ALL OF
THESE VERSES ARE IN THE
FIRST THREE CHAPTERS OF
THE BIBLE OR THE LAST
THREE CHAPTERS OF THE
BIBLE. GET A BOOKMARK OR
TWO, AND IT'LL GO MORE
QUICKLY THAN YOU THINK.
I DID A COUPLE TO GET
YOU STARTED.

Fill out the chart below by looking up the verses listed and describing the following elements.

	EDEN (GEN. 1–2)	EDEN AFTER SIN (GEN. 3)	NEW HEAVEN AND EARTH (REV. 20–22)
TREE OF LIFE	2:9 It was beautiful to look at and good to eat.	3:22-24 It became off limits because of sin.	22:2 It will flourish, providing fruit and healing.
FEATURES OF THE LAND	2:8-14 God planted a beautiful garden to provide for them.	3:17-19 The ground was cursed, filled with thorns and hard to work.	22:1-3 It will no longer be cursed but be fruitful and life-giving.
SATAN AND SIN	3:1	3:14-15	20:10; 21:27
BLESSING/ CURSE	1:28	3:16-19	21:4; 22:3
DEATH	2:16-17	3:20-24	20:14; 21:4
TOGETHERNESS WITH GOD	1:28; 2:8 God made a place for humanity to be together with Him.	3:8-10	21:3; 22:4

The new heaven and new earth will be such a far cry from "sitting on clouds with harps." It will be the culmination of every wonderful thing. And the core reason for being wonderful is not because of the features but because of the Father. Think about it: we won't just hear His sound in the garden like Adam and Eve did (Gen. 3:8,10), we will see His face (Rev. 22:4).

It reminds me of those videos of babies with impaired vision getting glasses. When they see their parents' faces for the first time, I ugly cry. It's so beautiful and sweet! I always wonder—when I finally see the Lord, who has loved me so well for so long, maybe it'll be like that.

What part of the new heaven and new earth do you most anticipate? What feels like the biggest relief right now? Explain.

According to 1 Thessalonians 4:16-18, we are to encourage one another with the promise of Jesus's return. After all, that's when every longing of our hearts will be fulfilled, and every horror of our lives will be redeemed. We will fully, finally, and forever be home— because we will be with God, and God will be with us.

LOOK UP REVELATION 22:20 **and write it below.**

This verse holds an important place in Scripture as the second-to-the-last verse in the Bible. Christians often say it when something terrible happens in the world. The words aren't a spiritual Band-Aid® but are something we express when the world's horrors leave us wordless even while we cling to God's promise. This phrase offers the world our greatest hope: Jesus is coming.

DAY FOUR
A SISTER'S STORY OF HOME

You may remember that Moses, a man who never really had a home, wrote in Psalm 90:1, "Lord, through all the generations you have been our home!" (NLT). Revelation 21:3 takes this true statement to the next level:

> I heard a loud shout from the throne, saying, "Look, God's home is now among his people! He will live with them, and they will be his people. God himself will be with them" (NLT).

Jesus is coming to make a new heaven and a new earth where we will fully, finally, and forever be with Him, safe from sin and death and enjoying true togetherness with our true family.

I want to share with you a letter from a fellow sister in Christ. As she shares her story of home, I hope it will point you to God's story of home and help you feel less alone in your own story.

Dear Friend,

It was December of my fourth-grade year. I ran home from school, elated because I had been cast in the lead role in my school Christmas play. I was finally getting a chance to be a part of something, to belong. See, that year had already been a bit of a roller coaster, and if I am honest all the years leading up to it were too. Our family had already moved four times that school year and about a dozen prior to that. I had not really had a chance to make friends or feel like a normal kid, but this play felt like a glimpse of normalcy. As I turned the corner onto our street my heart dropped. There was a moving truck in our driveway . . . again. I walked up on legs of stone, dreading what came next. Sure enough, we were moving. By the end of the weekend, we would be in a new home in a new state (the third one that year). By the end of that school year, we would be on our eighth move of the year and once again in a new state. I had completely stopped talking at school. I was so weary of trying to explain that—no, we weren't military; no, I wasn't a foster kid; no, we weren't running from the law; and no, I didn't think my parents were secretly spies. I just shut down and stopped trying to belong. In my experience, making friends just meant losing friends. A kid can only say so many goodbyes before you stop wanting to say hello.

Now in adulthood, I have lived in over fifty different places: houses, apartments, dorm rooms, and even briefly in my car. In all these places, I have never felt at home. I have been a wanderer in the wilderness, desperately seeking my promised land, my home, my place where I belonged both physically and in community. I have dreamt of a porch with creaking rocking chairs leading to a home chock-full of memories and loved ones. A place my children's children will always know as a haven, rooted in love. Instead, my life has been filled with moving boxes that never quite get fully unpacked and suitcases at the ready, because this is just another temporary stop.

I have cried out to God with weary tears asking, "When will I be home?" I have been frustrated at myself for not having patience in God's timing. I have also sat in awe as I look back at my journey, praising God for the epic adventures He has brought me through. God has blessed me with a husband that grew up with a completely different story, who reminds me that I am home if I am with my family. I have seen firsthand how my journey has equipped me with a strong ability to adapt and lean into the unwavering truth of God and His faithfulness to be at my side through it all.

The Lord has lovingly led me to His Word in the story of Moses. Moses was called on to lead his people through the wilderness for years just trying to reach the promised land. As he journeyed, he struggled, he had moments of wavering faith, he was weary, and he yearned to be home. But through this, he also experienced some epic moments. While Moses was kept from entering the promised land here on earth, he can rejoice in the eternal promised land. And in that same eternal promised land is a place for me. I can rest in knowing that all homes under the sun are temporary. I see how God is growing me, preparing me, and encouraging me toward true connection. Even in my impatience, God is faithful and—in His timing, in His design—I will have a home.

— SALINA KELLEY, Administrative
Assistant at Lifeway Women, Tennessee

Use the space below (or your own journal) to respond to this letter. You may want to use the following questions to guide your response.

What thoughts and feelings are you experiencing as you consider this sister's story?

What from her letter most resonates with you and why?

How does her story help you remember God's invitation to belong and be loved?

ALMOST HOME

To those His friends
Jesus promised two things
He would send a Helper,
And soon return as King

All the promises we've collected
Will be made manifest
We'll know it to be true
Every word that He said

So in faith we practice home
In faith we battle sin
That rises up between us
Especially what's within

It has no place among us
This temple where God lives
So as we walk by the Spirit
We repent, we forgive

When our steps get weary
We keep our gaze ahead
We wrap up in His promises
We cling to every thread

So sister, keep moving forward
You are almost home
With every shaking step
Know you're not alone

Soon He will return
To make all things right
No more tears or death
No more sin to fight

Every longing of your heart
Every piece of your story
Will all be made new
Will all become glory

Don't let your heart be troubled
Keep putting on the armor
It won't be long now
Home is just around the corner

The
STORY of
HOME

session seven

We've looked at God's story for the past six weeks, but as part of our final time together, I want to tell you the whole story in one swoop. The aim today isn't to study it but to step into it. I'm hoping this brief, narrative overview will help you *experience* God's story, make new connections to it, and love God and His Word even more deeply. I suggest you and the group you're studying with consider this time a "closing ceremonies" of sorts, a way to sear the story into your consciences, a way to step into the story beyond your place as Bible student but as a recipient of the promises. This is, of course, God's story—but in His goodness He decided it ought to be yours, too. This is *The Story of Home*.

GROUP GUIDE

session seven

COME ON IN

Plan some extra time this week to watch the full 20-minute teaching video. Instructions to access the videos can be found on page 160.

This final week is going to be a little different. As you watch the video, I'm going to be telling the story of home as one big story. This big story is the framework for each of our stories and helps us interpret the hows and whys of what's happening in our lives.

As you watch and listen, step into the story with me. Take notes below as we move through God's story of home and His promises to belong and be loved.

TAKE A SEAT

EDEN

ABRAHAM

MOSES

EXILE

JESUS

HOLY SPIRIT + JESUS'S RETURN

Use the following questions to reflect on what you've heard in the video teaching and discuss with your group:

What is one thing in the video teaching that stood out to you? Why?

How does hearing the story of home in Scripture told in one sitting help you better understand God's character and purpose?

Can you list the beautiful promises we have learned together over the last seven weeks? (If not, that's okay. Flip back to p. 120 for a quick refresh.)

Which promise have you most needed to hear and soak in as someone longing for home?

What is one thing you've learned in your journey home that you would like to pass on? Who will you share that with?

How do you need to apply what you've learned from this study?

We are not home yet, but we are on our way! God's invitation to belong and be loved is waiting for us right here and now. As we walk toward our true home, may we invite God to make us look more like Jesus every day. Close in prayer, thanking God that we will one day be fully, finally, and forever in perfect peace at home with Him.

LEADER GUIDE

ell

TIPS FOR LEADING A GROUP

PRAY DILIGENTLY. Ask God to prepare you to lead this study. Pray individually and specifically for the girls in your group. Make this a priority in your personal walk and preparation.

PREPARE ADEQUATELY. Don't just wing this. Take time to preview each week so you have a good grasp of the content. Look over the group session and consider those in your group. Feel free to delete or reword the questions provided, and add questions that fit your group better.

LEAD BY EXAMPLE. Make sure you complete all of the personal study. Be willing to share your story, what you're learning, and your questions as you discuss together.

BE AWARE. If girls are hesitant to discuss their thoughts and questions in a larger group, consider dividing into smaller groups to provide a setting more conducive to conversation.

FOLLOW UP. If someone mentions a prayer request or need, make sure to follow up. It may be a situation where you can get others in the group involved in helping out.

EVALUATE OFTEN. After each week and throughout the study, assess what needs to be changed to more effectively lead the study.

CONTENT NOTE: *Leaders, in a bonus video, Caroline reads a poem about someone she lost and the clip is understandably emotional. Consider what your girls are going through and if it's appropriate to watch the clip and read the poem on pages 144-149. We've also added a note on page 145 to girls walking through loss and grief. Read it aloud or point it out to them privately as you feel led.*

MAKE THE MOST OF YOUR GROUP TIME

If you are leading a Bible study group through *Come Home*, then first I want to say thank you! I have no doubt God will use you to encourage the girls in your group as you walk through His Word together. I can't wait to get started on this journey alongside you.

COME ON IN

At your first group meeting, watch the Session One intro video together and make sure all the girls in your group have their Bible study books. When you gather for Session Two, you'll discuss what you studied during the week and then watch the Session Two intro video together. It will be extremely helpful for you, as the leader, to watch the videos and read through the questions ahead of group time to prepare for discussion. **Please note:** Session Seven is a longer video (20 minutes) and will occupy the majority of your time together. Please don't skip this final week, but celebrate successfully spending seven weeks together walking toward God's invitation to belong and be loved.

TAKE A SEAT

Help ease into each session by starting off with some questions to get girls comfortable with one another. This opening section is also the perfect time to break out the snacks and some comfy seating options.

LET'S TALK

These questions and Scripture references are designed to bring deeper discussion. You are more than welcome to ask additional questions that you feel are important, or you can skip the questions we provided if your girls are owning the discussion with their own notes from the personal study. Bottom line: follow the Holy Spirit's leading as you enter this time.

LET'S PRAY

Before you end your time together, you will want to go over the personal study they should focus on before you meet again. Then, close out in prayer using the prayer practice as a way to encourage your girls before they are dismissed.

MOM & DAUGHTER GUIDE

Mom, we are so excited that you have decided to complete this study with your daughter. As Caroline Saunders walks you through the story of home, you will find an invitation for both you and your daughter to belong and be loved.

YOU WILL NEED

Come Home: Women's Bible Study Book for yourself

Come Home: Teen Girls' Bible Study Book for your daughter(s)

VIDEO CONTENT

The weekly videos that are included in the women's Bible study book can be watched with your daughter during the Group Guide sessions. Follow the instructions in the back of your women's Bible study book to access the teaching videos. Note: the videos included in the teen girl Bible study book are the introduction videos only to allow more time for discussion.

STUDY

At the close of each session, you will spend time working through the Group Time found in the *Come Home: Teen Girls' Bible Study Book*. The discussion questions will help you go deeper as you review your personal study and share what you've learned each week.

As you both work through your individual Bible study books, you will discover that the teen girls' version might be slightly different as we altered some language and content to be more applicable for teen girls. However, there are very few differences in the studies, and we encourage you to discuss what the Lord is teaching you individually.

CONNECT WITH HER

Plan days to work on personal study together to keep each other accountable. Be open with your daughter throughout the week about things you learn or have questions about. Provide a safe place for her to do the same. Don't stress! Some weeks will be easier than others to accomplish the personal study days. Just keep pressing forward and making it a priority to meet together each week regardless of how much personal study work was actually done.

FAQ

Q: How old does my teen need to be for this study?

A: This study is recommended for girls ages 11 and up.

Q: Are there other studies I can do with my daughter after this study is over?

A: Yes! Many of our studies have both women's and teen girls' materials available. Check it out at lifeway.com/girls.

PSST...IF YOU HAVE LITTLE ONES IN YOUR HOME, THEY MAY ENJOY CAROLINE'S CHILDREN'S BOOK, *THE STORY OF HOME*. AS THEY FLIP THROUGH THE PAGES, THEY CAN HUNT FOR THE HIDDEN SCRIPTURE REFERENCES, MANY OF WHICH YOU'LL ENCOUNTER WITHIN THIS BIBLE STUDY!

SPECIAL NOTE & POEM

Death and grief are very real and painful parts of our journey on the way home. Jesus dealt with them, and we will too. So, with caution, note that we'll be discussing death and grief in this short video and final poem.

If you're not in a place where you feel ready to watch the video clip or read the poem, feel free to skip pages 146-149 and just watch the main session video. Know that you are loved and seen and held, especially in this pain, by One who knows it well.

If you want to watch the video of the poem, scan the QR code below.

IF I COULD BUILD YOU A HOUSE

(A POEM FOR BAILEY)

If I could build a house
where pain couldn't root
where disease couldn't grow
where separation had no strength,
I would.
I would build it for you.

The roof would be firm in the storms
The walls would keep your body safe
The doors would say to pain,
"You are not welcome here."

In the garden, togetherness would grow
and it would not stop
It would cover the house like ivy
It would fill the space between us
like a fragrance
like the glow of a candle

We would pick the
togetherness like berries
We would serve it at our table
in big heaping bowls
We would store the extras in our cabinets
and it would spill out
everywhere. Everywhere.
With berry-stained hands,
we would laugh over the lovely mess
together. Together.

But togetherness doesn't grow like that,
not here.
Here we are apart.
Here my tools are faulty
Here my materials too weak
I would build it for you,
but I cannot.

Here tornadoes rip off roofs like a lid
Here doors can't keep out the pain and the hate
Here cancer grows where it was not planted
where it is not welcome
Here it takes what it was never given
And eats of the berries we so carefully collected
And smashes the space between us
This is not the house I would make for you.
If I could build another, I would
And yet, among these cracks and leaks
and these rusted hinges,
despite all the weak,
I notice something about our feet:
They are standing on something
strong.

I stomp and feel it firm beneath
Something built with hands not ours,
with tools not ours
Something built by Someone
who would build it
and could build it.
Someone who did not shut out pain
but welcomed it in,

who said to the winds and the disease
to the sin and the shame:
Come in my house instead.
Someone who surrendered His body
who gave up His home
who withheld not one cell
from the destruction we fear

And then from the ashy heap
He constructed this thing under
our feet
and despite all the shaking
it hasn't moved an inch.
Somehow in all the dying
the soil is still rich.
Somehow in all the separation
I can spot togetherness that grows
and cannot stop.

Darling, while much is lost
and much has been endured,
stomp and feel it firm beneath:
The foundation is unchanged.
No matter how our house shakes,
Nothing can stop this sprout of hope:
Of another home that our Builder is making

He is placing its foundation
In a place with no storms
Where you'll be perfectly safe
Where pain cannot come
because it does not know the way

A place with a garden where togetherness grows
and it cannot stop
It will cover the house like ivy
It will fill the space between us
like a fragrance
like the glow of a candle

In that house, one day,
we will pick the togetherness like berries
we will serve it at our table
in big heaping bowls

We will store the extras
in our cabinets
and it will spill out
everywhere. Everywhere.
With berry-stained hands,
we will laugh over the lovely mess
together. Together.

And our Builder will be there with us
(after all, it's His feast)
and we'll look at Him in awe, saying,
"We can't believe you made this!
We can't believe you made space for us!"
He'll stretch out His hands,
stained with blood and with berries,
draw us in close
and never let go.
Not ever. Not ever.

Written in honor and memory of my friend and former student Bailey Purkey, who passed away in 2020 of Small Cell Ovarian Cancer at twenty one years old.

ENDNOTES

Session One

1. Victor P. Hamilton, *The Book of Genesis, Chapters 1–17, The New International Commentary on the Old Testament* (Grand Rapids: Wm. B. Eerdmans Publishing Co., 1990), 192.

Session Two

1. BibleProject Podcast, "Wrestling God for a Blessing," February 14, 2022, in *BibleProject*, produced by Cooper Peltz, podcast, MPS audio, 1:06:23, https://bibleproject.com/podcast/wrestling-god-blessing/

2. M. G. Easton, *Illustrated Bible Dictionary and Treasury of Biblical History, Biography, Geography, Doctrine, and Literature* (New York: Harper & Brothers, 1893), 92,94.

3. Shamar: Strong's H8104, Bible Hub, accessed November 28, 2023, https://biblehub.com/hebrew/8104.htm.

4. Oxford Languages Dictionary, s.v. "better," accessed November 29, 2023, google.com.

Session Three

1. R. Dennis Cole, "Numbers," in *CSB Study Bible: Notes,* ed. Edwin A. Blum and Trevin Wax (Nashville, TN: Holman Bible Publishers, 2017), 219.

2. Steven J. Lawson, *Psalms 76–150*, ed. Max Anders, vol. 12, Holman Old Testament Commentary (Nashville, TN: Holman Reference, 2006), 81–82.

3. "What Was the Tabernacle?" Thomas Nelson Bibles blog, Adapted from the King James Study Bible, Full Color Edition, May 18, 2022, https://www.thomasnelsonbibles.com/blog/what-was-the-tabernacle/.

4. Elizabeth Woodson, *Embrace Your Life* (Nashville: B & H Publishing Group, 2022), 109.

Session Four

1. David W. Stowe, Song of Exile: *The Enduring Mystery of Psalm 137* (New York: Oxford University Press, 2016), 8.

2. "Ezekiel" in *The Jesus Bible,* ESV Edition (Grand Rapids, MI: Zondervan, 2019), 1236.

3. David Guzik, "Ezekiel 10 – The Glory and the Cherubim" in *The Enduring Word Bible Commentary*, (Goleta, CA: Enduring Word, 2021), https://enduringword.com/bible-commentary/ezekiel-10/.

4. Scott Aniol, "Musical Instruments," in *The Lexham Bible Dictionary*, ed. John D. Barry et al. (Bellingham, WA: Lexham Press, 2016).

5. Tim Keller, "Praying Our Anger," Gospel in Life, April 28, 2002, https://gospelinlife.com/downloads/praying-our-anger-5269/.

6. Paul Carter, "Dashing the Little Ones Against the Rock — Does this Verse Really Belong in Scripture," The Gospel Coalition, July 5, 2017, https://ca.thegospelcoalition.org/columns/ad-fontes/dashing-little-ones-rock-verse-really-belong-scripture/.

7. Paul Carter, "Dashing the Little Ones Against the Rock — Does this Verse Really Belong in Scripture," The Gospel Coalition, July 5, 2017, https://ca.thegospelcoalition.org/columns/ad-fontes/dashing-little-ones-rock-verse-really-belong-scripture/. https://ca.thegospelcoalition.org/columns/ad-fontes/dashing-little-ones-rock-verse-really-belong-scripture/

8. D Ralph H. Alexander, "Ezekiel," in *The Expositor's Bible Commentary: Isaiah, Jeremiah, Lamentations, Ezekiel*, ed. Frank E. Gaebelein, vol. 6 (Grand Rapids: Zondervan Publishing House, 1986), 754.

9. David W. Stowe, Song of Exile: *The Enduring Mystery of Psalm 137* (New York: Oxford University Press, 2016), 3.

10. Eugene H. Peterson, *Psalms: Prayers of the Heart: 12 Studies for Individuals or Groups: With Notes for Leaders* (Westmont, IL: IVP, 2000), 31.

11. BibleProject Podcast,, "The Significance of Seven," October 21, 2019, in *BibleProject*, produced by Dan Gummel, podcast, MPS audio, 1:05:33, https://bibleproject.com/podcast/wrestling-god-blessing/

12. David Guzik, "Daniel 9 – The Seventy Weeks of Daniel" in *The Enduring Word Bible Commentary*, (Goleta, CA: Enduring Word, 2018), https://enduringword.com/bible-commentary/daniel-9/.

Session Five

1. Genesis: Strong's G1078, Blue Letter Bible, accessed March 15, 2024, https://www.blueletterbible.org/lexicon/g1078/kjv/tr/0-1/.

2. Gerald L. Borchert, *John 1–11*, vol. 25A, The New American Commentary (Nashville: Broadman & Holman Publishers, 1996), 119–120.

3. Sympatheō: Strong's G4834, Blue Letter Bible, accessed November 29, 2023, https://www.blueletterbible.org/lexicon/g4834/kjv/tr/0-1/.

4. Andreas J. Kostenberger and Alexander E. Stewart, *The First Days of Jesus* (Wheaton: Crossway, 2015), 140.

Session Six

1. Encyclopaedia Britannica, s.v. "cornerstone," by The Editors of Encyclopaedia Britannica, accessed March 18, 2024, https://www.britannica.com/technology/cornerstone.

2. "1 Peter," *The Jesus Bible*, (Grand Rapids: Zondervan, 2019), 1870.

3. Randy Alcorn, "Forever: Made for a Different Place," *The Jesus Bible*, (Grand Rapids: Zondervan, 2019), 1938.

4. Nancy Guthrie, *Even Better Than Eden*, (Wheaton: Crossway, 2018).

Other Studies from
Caroline Saunders
for Teen Girls

Better Than Life: How to Study the Bible and Like It
An in-depth study of Psalm 63 to help you learn to study the Bible and delight in God's Word.

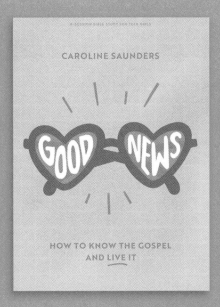

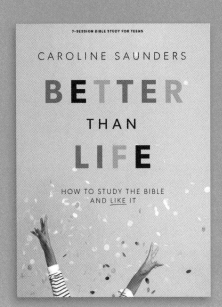

Good News: How Know the Gospel and Live It
Discover the good news of the gospel, not just for eternity but for today, too!

YOU
BELONG,
and YOU ARE
LOVED

NOTES

NOTES

NOTES

NOTES

NOTES

Come Home

NOTES

Get the most from your study.

Customize your Bible study time with a guided experience.

In this study you'll:

- Unpack the theme of home found throughout Scripture.
- Identify your spiritual homesickness and be equipped to process your longing for home through God's story.
- Understand how God's promise of a true, forever home is better than any home we have experienced.

HOW TO WATCH YOUR VIDEOS

1. **Go to** my.lifeway.com/redeem **and register or log in to your Lifeway account.**

2. **Enter this redemption code to gain access to your individual-use video license:**

YVF4H8CKKYX8

Once you've entered your personal redemption code, you can stream the video teaching sessions any time from your Digital Media page on my.lifeway.com or watch them via the Lifeway On Demand app on any TV or mobile device via your Lifeway account.

There's no need to enter your code more than once! To watch your streaming videos, just log in to your Lifeway account at my.lifeway.com or watch using the Lifeway On Demand app.

eBook with video access, includes 7 intro teaching sessions from Caroline Saunders, each approximately 3-5 minutes

Bible Study for Women includes video access to 7 video teaching sessions from Caroline Saunders

Browse study formats, a free session sample, leader assets, and more at lifeway.com/comehome

QUESTIONS? WE HAVE ANSWERS!

Visit support.lifeway.com and search "Video Redemption Code" or call our Tech Support Team at 866.627.8553.